SUCKING CHEST WOUND

DANIEL J. VOLPE

COPYRIGHT

Edited by Mary Danner
Paperback cover by Brian Csati
Formatted by Matt Wildasin
Publisher Bad Dream Books

ISBN: 978-1-961758-17-9

SUCKING CHEST WOUND

MORE WORKS FROM DANIEL J. VOLPE:

Billy Silver
Awakened in Blood
Talia
Talia 2: Halls of Blood
A Gift of Death
Black Hearts and Red Teeth
Left to You
For the Better
Sew Sorry (with Aron Beauregard)
Through the Eyes of Desperation: The Black Version
A Story of Sorrow: Books 1-3
Only Psychos
Plastic Monsters
Multiple Stab Wounds

TABLE OF CONTENTS

SUCKING CHEST WOUND

The cops had dogs with them; Andy fucking hated dogs. He'd fight the pigs all day if any of them were man enough to stand toe-to-toe with him, but he *hated* dogs.

Andy Lakken ran, not quite panicked, but with a purpose. The leaves were wet under his feet, and it seemed like every root or stick found his muddy boots. It didn't help that it was dark, with only a sliver of the moon peeking out.

After ten years of perfecting his craft, he'd finally been caught. It took them a while to figure out it was him—a virus moving from town to town with murder on the mind, but he slipped up and gave the pigs the break they needed.

Andy wasn't greedy. He'd kill one or two kids, usually latch-key boys and girls, and leave their mutilated bodies in shallow graves on his way out of town. It was something he loved, something he was good at. He didn't know *why*, though.

His parents loved him; they didn't beat him or his sister. He grew up with friends and was good looking enough to have had girlfriends since grade school. But no amount of pussy or blowjobs filled the void inside him. For a while, he thought maybe he was gay, or just didn't like sex. Of course, it felt great, but there was no excitement in it. Even the risky stuff—public fucking, unprotected sex, and some of the kinky shit—didn't do it for him. All he could think about was what they'd look like dead.

During a blowjob, he imagined his cock as the barrel of a gun, and when he'd cum, it wasn't his load hitting the back of her throat, it was a bullet. Andy would think of her (it didn't matter which girl, they were all the same to him) dead, with brains all over the wall. Every time he fucked and saw the look of pleasure on his partner's face, he imagined what their tortured grimace would look like. Would it be similar as he slowly inserted blades between their toes? Would they moan like they did when his cock entered them if a drill bit pierced bone?

He had killed animals—that was child's play. Every creature, be it domestic or wild, felt his wrath, but killing them was akin to masturbating. Yes, it felt good, but it wasn't the same as doing it with a person.

The first person he killed was a young prostitute. It was the best day of Andy's life. She stood, scared, under the sodium lights of a truck stop. It was a cold night in the Northeast, with a snowstorm on the horizon.

***

Andy wasn't a trucker, but he knew the lots could be ripe for targets. At that stage in his desire for murder, he didn't care if it was man or woman, he just needed someone easy. He didn't think an over-the-road trucker would be missed until their load was late, and by that time, Andy would be two states over, nestled in his childhood bed—the same bed with posters of Arnold Schwarzenegger fighting the Predator above it.

The girl was wandering the lot. She couldn't have been older than twenty, but he guessed she might have been in her late teens; a runaway, more than likely.

The impending storm sent most of the trucks scrambling, heading west. Only a few of the behemoths idled, rumbling with a growl like a monster. But *they* weren't the monsters, *Andy* was.

He sat in his car—a non-descript Japanese sedan he stole from the long-term lot at the airport. "Take my Breath Away" played on the radio, and Andy smiled at the irony of the new pop song. He hadn't seen the movie *Top Gun* yet, but was considering treating himself if he followed through with his plan.

Though he wasn't a smoker, he wished he was. His nerves were rattled, but Andy knew it was time for him to express himself in a way very few people would understand. Slowly, he drove through the lot toward the girl who hugged herself under the light, a cigarette burning between her fingers.

"You look cold," Andy said as he stopped next to her. He turned the dome light on so she could see he looked nice.

The prostitute leaned down and looked in the car. She took a drag of her cigarette and blew the smoke away from the open window. "I'm freezing my tits off," she said, with just a hint of humor in her voice.

Andy smiled and looked at the tits she referred to. Decent, but nothing too big. Maybe he'd cut them off after he killed her. The jury was still out on that one.

"Well, it's pretty warm in here," he said, gesturing to the passenger seat. "But I'm sure we can warm it up even more."

Up close, Andy could see the wear on her face. Her makeup was caked but looked days old. Her eyes were bloodshot and her hair was dirty. She hadn't seen a decent shower in a while, and there was just the hint of body odor mingled with the wafting smoke. She was perfect.

"You read my mind," she said, tossing the cigarette butt onto the litter-strewn lot. She walked around to the passenger side and got in, bringing with her the smell of smoke, cheap perfume, and her unwashed musk. "I'm Megan."

Andy put the car in drive and pulled away. He didn't think any of the remaining truckers had seen him, or even given a fuck, but he wanted to leave as soon as he could.

"Andy." There was no need for an alias; she would not be alive for much longer anyway.

Before he picked her out, Andy found the spot where he'd kill her. It wasn't far, but it was desolate, a dead-end road which looked like a failed project from ages past. It was chained off, but Andy cut that before picking her up.

They drove to the end of the road and Andy turned the car around, facing the way they came. He killed the lights, but kept the car running.

"So, what can I do for you?" Megan asked. Her hand was on his lap, stroking his cock.

Andy was already hard. It wasn't arousal for sex, but for murder. It was a different excitement; one he never felt before. He was scared. Not for the act of killing, but for the monster he was becoming—addicted to pain and death, snatching the life from others to satiate his desires.

Megan unzipped his jeans and teased the slick head of his penis. "Do you want me to suck it? That's my specialty. And I won't even make you wear a rubber. You can dump your load in my mouth. I'll even swallow it."

The only thing Andy wanted her to swallow was her own blood.

His hand snapped out and grabbed her chin and squeezed her face, not too hard, but enough to startle her. "No, I want that pussy. I want you bent over the hood of the car."

Reluctantly, he let go of her. His fingers left small dimples in her flesh. There was fear there, but he knew she'd been through worse; he could see it in her eyes.

Megan opened the door, letting the cold back in. She shivered, but obliged.

Andy slid out of his open door. He wanted to grab his knife, but the last thing he needed was to be covered in her blood. This was his life—taking others—and he couldn't get caught, especially the first time around.

He would do this one clean, feel her life fade through his body. Her pulse would spike from fear, and drop from impending death, while his would be pinned like the tachometer in a racecar the entire time. Andy was aroused like he'd never been before. Sex suddenly had meaning to him.

Megan was leaning against the hood of the car, facing him. She was cold, but she didn't know she was about to become room-temperature.

"Turn around and bend over," Andy said as he grabbed her by the arm.

A glimpse of fear shone in her eyes at that moment. It was fleeting, but Andy saw it. She knew him for what he was: a predator. It could've been the too-strong grip he had on her thin upper arm, or the growl in his voice. Lust was in his actions, but so was violence. She sensed it like any prey animal would, but she turned.

Megan put her hips against the warm hood of the car and reached underneath her skirt. She lowered her underwear and looked back at Andy, who was already working his cock from his jeans.

"There's a condom in my purse," Megan said, grabbing her bag from the hood. She plucked a prophylactic from the dark hole that was her life-line and handed it back to Andy.

He looked at it for a moment, then took it from her. There was no need for it. Andy wanted to feel her, all of her, and feeling someone die from the inside was his new dream. He would not let a ten-cent gas station rubber ruin that for him.

Andy tore open the package and pretended to put the condom on. Having her at ease would make things go smoother. He didn't need her scared until the last minute.

"All set," he said, then grabbed her bony hips and pulled her away from the hood, giving her more room to bend over.

There wasn't much to see in the dark, but he could smell her unwashed ass and pussy. She'd smell much worse in a day or two when the rot started creeping into her flesh and gut.

Andy spit on his hand and fished around in the darkness, coating her sex with his saliva.

Megan quivered at his touch, but quickly settled down. She may have been young, but that was her job. The faster things ended, the faster she got paid.

He rammed himself into her without warning.

She let out a small shriek and a gasp as Andy impaled her.

Soon, their juices mingled, creating a slick playground. It was obvious he wasn't wearing a condom, especially to a prostitute, but Megan didn't complain.

In the dim light of the moon, Andy's bare ass shone white as he bucked. His orgasm was on the horizon. It was the moment of truth.

Megan's neck was covered with her hair. Her hands were on the hood of the car, bracing against his thrusts.

He let go of her waist and wrapped his left arm around her neck. He'd never strangled anyone before. Not knowing what to expect, he squeezed as hard as he could.

Megan's hands shot up to grab at his arm, but the pressure Andy had on her windpipe and arteries was like a vice. She gurgled and fought.

Andy continued to fuck and strangle. He wished he could see her face: the fear, the pain, and the hopelessness of the end of her life.

The fight was leaving her. Consciousness was fading, as was her breath.

He was cumming. He rammed himself deep into her, unleashing his spunk into her dying pussy. At that moment, Andy's life changed forever. That wasn't just sex or murder, it was something different. It was as if he traveled through the stars to find the meaning of life. Fuck love, that was nonsense; *this* was what life was about.

Warmth ran from Megan, and Andy didn't know if it was urine or his jizz, or possibly a mixture of both, as her life ended on a dead-end street near the truck stop.

Andy shuddered as the final pulse of pleasure left his body. He was drained. His arm was sore from strangling Megan, and he realized he kept the same tight hold.

She fell hard when he released her, hitting the ground lifeless and violated.

Staggering like he was drunk, Andy spun and put his bare ass on the warm hood of the car. A pearl of cum bloomed from his swollen cock as it pointed toward the heavens.

Megan's dead eyes looked up at the same stars, taking in the clouds and dull moon. Eyes that saw their last sunrise, a gaping mouth that tasted its last morsel of food, and a heart that had pumped its last drop of blood, all in a lifeless heap on the ground at the end of an unused road.

Andy bent down to pull his pants up and noticed one of Megan's breasts had become exposed in the fight. The creamy skin looked beautiful in the moonlight. Her nipple contrasted the flesh and called to him. Andy crouched, his cock pointing at her like a divining rod seeking death. He touched her chest and felt something stir. His night wasn't over, not yet.

He kicked off his pants, which were around his ankles, and went back to the car.

When he came back, in his hand was a knife, and on his face was a smile.

***

That was ten years ago. Since, Andy grew a little heavier, a little older, and was on the run, sprinting through a patch of woods. Over the years, he'd killed up and down the east coast, leaving raped and mutilated corpses in his wake. He was invincible, or so he thought.

Andy, using his poor judgment and lack of forethought, kept one of them alive. She would not stay that way for very long, just enough for him to torture her to his liking, but the clever bitch escaped.

A branch whipped him in the face. Warm blood ran down his cheek, but he didn't dare stop. He could hear the barking of the dogs in the distance. They were on his trail. His best bet was to outrun them, try to get ahead of their dragnet and into the clear.

So fucking stupid!

He let the girl see him day in and day out as he took pieces of her. Andy could only hope her traumatized mind was too battered to identify him, but that was a long shot.

Andy slipped again. It rained the day before, and the air was full of cool moisture. He was cold and sweaty, each breath was painful and strained. Nevertheless, he pushed on. The sound of his racing pulse echoed in his ears, but he heard something else: a voice.

"Fuck me," he grumbled, looking around.

There was no one else nearby, but then he saw the flicker of a flashlight to his left.

"No, no, no," he said.

Their net had closed a little more. The cops and the dogs were at his back, and another set of pigs was waiting for him. It was a classic fucking ambush—one Andy was running headlong into.

He turned and franticly ran away from them. Never did he think he'd get caught at such a young age. He thought maybe he'd continue his reign of terror into his elder years, maybe even have some kids (if he could keep himself from killing their mother) to pass along his genes for the love of murder.

Andy charged forward, looking over his shoulder, and didn't see the jagged branch sticking out right at chest level. The sharp piece of wood entered his ribcage, breaking bone and piercing his lung.

Reacting to the violation of his body, he spun away, yanking the stick free. The air rushed out of Andy's lung, and he felt like he had a collapsed balloon in his chest. Stumbling, slipping, and injured, he fell. The soft flesh of his palms met jagged rock and wet earth.

He pushed himself up to his feet, but the wind was gone. His breath was non-existent. Darting forward into the darkness, panicked, Andy slipped again, but there was nothing under his feet.

Blackness enveloped him as he plummeted. Hard ground caught him moments later, but his momentum carried him. Bloodied hands reached to slow his descent, but they couldn't find purchase. In the moonlight, Andy saw what awaited him below: a river.

"Fuck!" Andy yelled, much louder than he intended, as he splashed into the rushing water.

***

Spring Break was JJ's favorite time of the year. Most kids yearned for summer vacation or Christmas break, but JJ loved the spring.

It was a time of rebirth, where things came out of the cold ground and into the warmth of the sunlight. The dead rose, withered limbs returning to vibrant green. Birds chirped as they returned from their winter escape to the warmer weather of the southern states.

For JJ, it was special for multiple reasons. His mother worked for the school district, so while the kids were off, the staff had to work. They received some vacation days, but not nearly as many as the kids. Their superintendent graciously gave them a four-day weekend, while the kids had the entire time off.

JJ's father was an over-the-road trucker, and was gone most of the year. JJ always figured it was because he hated them, which was partially true. There was no abuse or anything like that, but there was certainly no love either, so he never felt close to his father.

It didn't help that JJ's younger brother, Daryl, was slow. He wasn't an invalid, but even at eleven, Daryl had trouble with simple things such as tying his shoes, or remembering to take his underwear down before he shit. It wasn't every time, but now and again, Daryl would walk around with a turd in his pants.

Some kids took to calling him 'Dirty Daryl' or just 'Shit'. Well, that was until JJ got a hold of them.

JJ wasn't big, but at thirteen, he wasn't small either. He stood over five feet and was whip thin with knuckles that seemed harder than most. His bones were just the same as everyone else's, but when most kids would punch, they'd take a little off it. Not JJ, he hit you full force. He wanted it to hurt. He *loved* when it hurt, and hurting things was one reason JJ loved Spring Break.

With his dad away and his mom at work, there was no one to watch Daryl. His parents certainly wouldn't leave JJ in charge of the special needs boy, so they had no choice but to find a sitter for him. But JJ was more than capable of being left alone, at least during the day, or so his parents thought. If only they knew what their son was doing. If only they knew what he did during the spring of '96.

***

They didn't have a name for the little group even though that seemed like the popular thing to do. There were only three of them, so giving themselves a name seemed kind of stupid. It didn't matter, they were *his* crew. No leader had been established in a formal sense, but in the hierarchy of teen boys, everyone knew who the alpha was.

And that alpha was JJ.

Matt and Nick had no problem with that. They didn't mind being followers, even if JJ did some questionable things. It wasn't like they'd gotten in trouble or anything, at least not yet. JJ always had a plan and seemed to have a way out of everything. Even if the other two boys didn't quite agree with JJ's ideas, they still went along with him. What other choice did they have?

Their neighborhood was a decent size, but most of the other boys were either older or younger. As much as they wanted to fit in with the older boys, they couldn't. Their priorities were different. At thirteen, they were still in the phase of running off in the woods, turning over rocks, and pretending. At sixteen, the older boys were trying to feel a tit, or even get laid, or at least lie about it.

JJ, Nick, and Matt were it. They were a trio of thirteen-year-old boys with an entire week of Spring Break ahead of them. A week of freedom to run in the woods, ride bikes, and get into trouble.

JJ loved trouble. No one could prove he killed Mrs. Heater's cat, but she looked at him funny whenever she saw him.

Nick and Matt didn't know what to think the day they showed up at his house and he had the orange tabby in a cage.

JJ was filling a garbage can with a hose when they walked into the garage.

"Doing chores?" Matt asked.

He was a little on the pudgy side, but as tall as JJ. JJ's dad said Matt would sprout like a weed in the next few years and be a monster. JJ didn't see it. He knew his friend was soft, regardless of how big he grew to be.

Matt adjusted his glasses as he noticed the angry cat in the cage.

"Is that Mrs. Heater's cat?" Nick asked.

Nick was vanilla ice cream, plain as could be. Average height, average weight, nothing special about him. He was just there. If he ran away, nobody would even bother putting his face on a flyer.

"Yeah. This fucking cocksucker killed a bird and left it on the porch. I nearly shit my pants," JJ lied.

In reality, he hated the cat and baited it from his neighbor's yard to his using old lunch meat. A big pile of slimy cold cuts awaited the beast in the trap he'd hidden under the back porch.

Nick looked at the hissing cat as it swiped at him from inside its prison. "He's pretty pissed off."

JJ turned off the hose, which was connected to the slop sink faucet. "I'd be too if I had a belly full of rotten meat and was about to die."

Matt gave him a crooked smile, but JJ could tell he was nervous. He knew them both well enough to tell when they were scared, and he scared them a lot.

"Whadaya mean?" Matt looked at him, and finally put two and two together. "You're going to drown him?"

JJ smiled and tossed the leaky hose in the sink. "No, *we're* going to drown him."

"Fuck yeah, I hate cats," Nick said, but the waver in his voice betrayed his fear.

"We're not gonna waste the opportunity for a little friendly wager, right?" JJ asked.

The other boys looked at him confused.

"We'll bet on how long it takes for the little fucker to die. Five bucks each and the winner takes all."

Matt picked at a dirty fingernail. He tore it to the cuticle and tossed it on the dirty floor. "I don't have much time, JJ." His lying skills were shitty, which was why JJ hoped the chubby kid never became a criminal. He'd bend over quicker than a cheap whore. "And…and I really don't mind cats. I've had Mittens since I was a baby, and she's pretty cool." A thin sheen of sweat glistened on his forehead.

"It's okay," JJ said. "If you're a pussy, just say so."

Nick laughed. "Yeah, a big ole hairy pussy. I'm sure you're nice and fishy, right, pussy?" He raised a hand to high-five JJ, but he wasn't paying attention.

The leader of their little group was watching Matt's large eyes behind the lenses of his glasses. JJ licked his lips. He knew Matt would crumble; he always did.

Without breaking his gaze, Matt reached into his back pocket and pulled out his wallet. The Velcro protested when he peeled it open to remove a crumpled five-dollar bill. "I'm saying he doesn't last past a minute."

JJ smiled and pulled his money from his pocket. "Atta boy. I'll give the little fucker forty-five seconds, tops."

Both of them looked at Nick, who was the new target. Oh, how quickly things turn.

Frantically, he dug in his pants. "I only have three bucks," he said, holding onto the crumpled wad of singles. "I'm good for it if I lose. A minute and ten seconds is my bet."

JJ took the money from both boys, combining it with his own. He pocketed it and picked up the trap.

The cat hissed and spat, reaching through the bars to scratch its captors.

"Okay, you little cocksucker, make daddy some money." Without another word, JJ dropped the trap into the garbage can.

The flailing and bubbles lasted a minute and a half.

That wasn't the first animal JJ had killed, but it was the first time he'd included the other two in his plans. He had to test them to see where their loyalty was. When he snuck out that night and tossed the water-logged cat in the backyard of his bitch neighbor, he knew the other boys wouldn't rat on him. It was mutually assured destruction if they did. They were just as guilty, and he made sure they knew it.

Mrs. Heater bitched and moaned about the cat, but couldn't prove anything. It rained the night before, so the cat being wet wasn't an issue. Still, the old cunt knew it was JJ. She just couldn't prove it.

That was how he'd kicked off his summer vacation the year prior. With spring beginning, he was ready to start anew, yearning for a new year of trouble.

***

The spring morning was cool. It was one of those days of perfection, at least to JJ. The morning air was crisp, with a wetness about it, but the lurking warmth of the afternoon was just around the corner.

JJ, Matt, and Nick met at the entrance to the woods. It was the meet-up spot they'd used hundreds of times to begin their days.

"What did you bring?" JJ asked the other two boys as they approached him.

Each of them had an old backpack slung over their shoulders. To the layman, their packs carried nothing more than nonsense: plastic bottles, bits of old shirts, some rope, a battered comic book or two, and a hastily made sandwich. But to the boys, these were treasures. They were adventurers, and their packs carried their lives in them.

JJ's contained similar items, with the same collection of randomness. He'd been able to swipe a few firecrackers and an old lighter with just barely a hint of fluid in it. The firecrackers were cool, but the cream of the crop was the knife. He purposely didn't tell his friends about it, wanting them to see it on his hip when they walked up.

The day before, JJ stumbled upon a yard sale. It wasn't much, but he was intrigued, as any thirteen-year-old boy looking for random treasure would be. When he saw the old blade, his heart skipped a beat. His parents had given him a small pocketknife when he was little, but that thing was so dull, even JJ couldn't get an edge on it. It sat buried in a box full of other discarded things he'd outgrown.

The knife at the yard sale was not a kid's toy; it was six inches of cold steel. A fixed blade too, not some dinky folding knife that could close on your fingers and slice you. It was a fighting knife, something made to kill.

The owners of the house watched the curious boy look at their wares, but JJ knew they wouldn't sell it to him. Plus, he didn't have a single penny on him. He was going to steal it, but with their watchful glares, it was impossible until a few more patrons came looking for a bargain.

Without thinking twice, when the time was right, JJ stole the knife from the table, hopped onto his bike, and pedaled away.

It hung from his hip in its leather sheath. JJ rested his hand on the pommel of the knife, drawing attention to it.

Matt and Nick were just about to tell him what they had in their bags when Nick saw the knife.

"Oh shit, where'd you get that?" Nick asked.

Matt, seeing the knife and the smile on JJ's face, rushed over to examine the deadly tool.

JJ pulled the knife from its sheath, letting the blade shimmer in the sunlight. "I stole it." He had no issues telling his buddies about his theft. They'd done much worse than stealing from a yard sale.

Both boys looked at him in awe, their gazes going from his blue eyes to the glimmering blade.

"Yeah, I figured it was time for us to have a *real* knife, not some bullshit kiddie blade." JJ swiped it through the air a few times, letting the other two hear the *swoosh* it made, cutting nothing. With just a bit of flourish, he tucked the blade back into its sheath. "Come on, let's get going. I want to hit the river before it gets too late. See if we can catch something for lunch."

The woods were their haven. Sunlight shone down, filtering through the green above. Pockets of brightness found holes in the foliage, dotting the terrain in pools of gold. Animals moved and spoke, giving the forest a voice. The boys moved and spoke as well, talking all sorts of nonsense that boys talk; silence was not welcome in their world at that moment.

Bits of laughter and jokes carried on the spring air. The sun rose higher, chasing away some of the morning chill. In their youthful bliss, they strayed from the path, taking in the beauty of the woods. They were in no rush, as they knew the river would be there when they arrived. The only thing moving them along was the hunger in their bellies, but even that was put on the back burner as they explored.

Finally, after they had their fill of climbing trees and flipping rocks, they continued their trek. The morning chill was gone, replaced by the growing warmth of the noon sun. In the distance, they heard the sound they'd been waiting for: the river.

It wasn't a massive body of water, but for the boys, it was heaven. They spent a good chunk of their summers damming a portion of the river, creating a deep pool. It was just enough for them to sit and cool themselves from the oppressive summer heat. The rest of the river flowed freely, coming to a bend right by the clearing they'd made over the years. It was a perfect spot to fish and drop crawfish traps.

They all unshouldered their packs and sat around the makeshift fire pit, which was just a rudimentary ring of rocks. Without speaking, they built a small pile of sticks on top of the cold ash.

"Gonna be a warm one today," Matt said, as he wiped the sweat from his brow. He dug into his pack and pulled out an old Zippo lighter.

It didn't matter how warm it was outside, they needed some kind of fire; it didn't feel right being in the woods without it.

He touched the flame to the dry kindling, catching it alight. The flame ate and snaked through the dry wood with ease.

Nick sipped from a canteen he pulled from his bag. "Yeah, it's supposed to be nearly eighty or so." With the back of his hand, he wiped the sweat from his face, but still sat near the fire. He raised the canteen back to his lips and stopped. "What the hell is that?" His finger was rigid, pointing into the trees, getting the attention of the other boys.

JJ and Matt looked where their friend was pointing. At first, the boys only saw trees, but JJ noticed something else.

"I think that's a body," JJ said. He was standing, using his dirty hand to shield his eyes from the sun. Without waiting for the other two, he darted into the woods toward the lump at the bank of the river.

Branches whipped at his face, but JJ didn't let that slow him. He heard the other boys on his tail. They were yelling for him to wait up, but he didn't listen. If it was a dead body, he had to see it first. JJ wanted to take it all in alone—to be the first to witness the rot and decay, the first to smell the putrescence of water-logged, fish-eaten human meat. Part of him figured it was going to be nothing more than a pile of trash washed ashore. The closer he got, he realized it was a live person, not a dead body.

Against a tree sat a man. He was wet and shivering, but that wasn't what caught JJ's eye; it was the blood. The man's chest was covered in red, and his face was pale.

He looked up at JJ when the boy came to a halt only a few feet from him. "Hey there, bud. A little help, maybe? Ya got some food, or water, or maybe something to plug this hole in my chest?" the wounded man said. He grinned, but it was pained.

Matt and Nick came up to the pair. All three boys breathed heavily, but their excitement and adrenaline chased away the exertion of their lungs.

"Holy shit!" Matt said. His hand was on his side trying to rub away a stomach cramp. "Who the fuck is this?" he asked his friends, as if the three of them didn't just stumble across the wounded man together. "Who the fuck are you?" he asked the man. "And what happened to your chest?"

Nick squinted, staring at the man with a bit of recognition on his face. They locked eyes, and then the man winked.

"Oh fuck, I know who he is. I saw his picture on the news last night," Nick said. He looked at his friends, grabbing them by the arms.

"Huh, is he a celebrity or somethin'?" Matt asked.

JJ squatted on his haunches and looked at the man. He didn't just look, but really *saw* him; he saw something in him he'd seen in himself. "No, he's not a celebrity. At least, to normal people, he isn't. He's a killer, aren't you, buddy?"

The man smiled with blood on his lips.

"Lakken, Andy Lakken, right?" Nick asked. He looked at the damage to Andy's chest. "And it looks like you got a sucking chest wound." Before anyone could ask how he knew that, he added, "My dad was a medic for years. He talked a lot when he drank."

"Guilty," Andy said. "They've said terrible things about me on the news." His grin widened, though it looked like it was causing him pain. "And for the most part, they're all true." His wound hissed when he breathed.

"Whoa," all three boys said.

They were face-to-face with a bona fide serial killer.

"Hey!" Nick said, looking at the other boys. "There's a reward for catching killers, right? We need to turn him in and get paid. Do you know how rich we could be?"

Matt nodded. "Yeah, you see that all the time. The rewards are huge."

JJ let them talk. Money interested him, but he had been given a golden opportunity, something that far outweighed cash: the chance to talk with a killer, to pick his brain, find out why he existed. Learn why JJ had the urges to kill, and if there was any way he could ever defeat it, or how to avoid getting caught. It was the chance to learn from a master.

JJ's mind was racing. He knew his friends had big mouths and would tell as soon as they made it back home. The thought of easy money and glory was too much for them. They couldn't see the opportunity in front of them. They couldn't, but JJ could, and he was their leader.

"Hey," JJ said to Matt, "do you have any rope in your bag?"

Matt looked up in thought. "Yeah, I think so."

"Good. Go back and grab it."

Matt nodded and ran back toward their make-shift little camp.

"Hey bud, what are you doing?" asked Andy. "I don't much need rope, but some help. I'm sure three strong boys could help me to my feet and out of these woods." With each word he spoke, more blood trickled down his shirt. A wheezing sound came from the ragged hole in his chest.

"No, you're not going anywhere, pal," JJ said.

Matt came back to join them holding a short length of rope in his hand. It was more than enough to tie someone's wrists with.

Andy looked at JJ. Their eyes locked and a flash of recognition shot across the face of the wounded man.

JJ gasped, but just slightly. What he saw in Andy, Andy saw in him.

"Okay, you're in charge, big man," Andy said, with a bit of humor in his voice.

JJ drew the knife from the sheath on his hip. "You're damn right I am." He looked at Matt. "Tie his hands."

Matt suddenly looked terrified, like he shrunk in on himself and was a little boy once again who feared the dark. He looked at Nick, who watched the entire encounter.

"Wh-why? He's hurt," Matt said. "It's not like he's gonna go anywhere."

"Do you want the prize money?" JJ asked. The money was leaving his thoughts, but something more devious was taking its place.

"Well yeah, but—" Matt started.

"No fucking buts," JJ said, pointing the knife at his friend. "This guy is a killer and worth a ton of money. Who knows, he could be faking his injury. Or playing it off like it's worse than it really is. Maybe he's just resting and then is going to head into town. Do you want him to come to your house and kill your mom?"

Matt and Nick both looked like scolded children.

"No," Nick said.

"That's what I thought. Let's tie his ass up." JJ pointed the knife back at Andy.

Matt and Nick apprehensively moved closer to the bloody killer. Matt's hands shook.

"Try anything funny, and I'll stick you," JJ said. His voice didn't waver, and he meant what he said. Part of him hoped the man tried something. He wondered what it would be like to feel those inches of cold steel enter a human body.

"Lean forward," Nick ordered.

Andy listened to Nick, but didn't take his eyes off JJ. With a little more haste than necessary, Matt tied Andy's hands together behind his back.

"There, are you happy?" Andy asked. "Now, can I have a fucking drink or maybe a bite of food?"

Matt opened his bag and began fishing around.

"No," JJ said. "Fuck him. He's a killer." He turned his gaze back to the wounded man. "He doesn't get shit."

They hadn't realized it, but the sun was already dipping in the sky. "Let's go back and tell the cops. Then we can get some reward money," Nick said.

"Hell yeah," Matt added.

JJ didn't speak. The other two boys looked at him, but JJ was staring at Andy like they were in a test of wills.

"JJ, are you good?"

JJ broke his gaze, but Andy still watched him with a vulpine grin. "Yeah, let's get the fuck out of here." He sheathed the knife as the other two boys started walking away. JJ was slower, but moving.

"You're not like them. They sense it, but don't know it for certain. They're scared of you, aren't they? You've done things that have put fear into them, but they won't admit it. You, mister JJ, are like me—a predator." Andy stopped and took a gasping breath. The hole in his chest oozed blood, but it wasn't flowing fast.

JJ swallowed hard. It felt like he had a cotton ball in his throat. No, he wasn't like the man in front of him. At least, he didn't think he was.

Liar!

Yes, yes, he was. He yearned to take a life, a human life. Every day, he stared into that void, gazing at the inky blackness of himself. How easy would it be to kill a person? *As simple as cutting a steak*, he thought. Or better yet, getting one of his father's deer rifles and blowing someone's head off. He'd seen what those big bullets did to a deer, so he knew the power behind them. That seemed cheap. To shoot someone wasn't his way, if he had a way. A blade or his bare hands were his ways. He wanted to witness the fear in the face of his victim, to see their pain as they realized life was over and their last memories would be of him.

JJ didn't talk, he just listened. He took it all in and looked in on himself. "Enjoy your night."

"JJ, let's go!" Nick yelled from where they left their stuff.

"I'll see you soon, JJ," Andy said, but the boy was darting off into the trees.

***

The boys melted into the trees and, once again, Andy was alone. Well, physically he was, but in his mind, he was never alone. The souls of each kill stayed with him, lounging in his brain, talking with him. They each provided him with calmness and joy. Even with the collapsed lung and pain, he felt some solace knowing how many souls he'd claimed in his lifetime.

He knew the boy, JJ, would be back. There was something dark in that one. A kindred spirit who had the look and feel of a killer. There was no conscience behind those eyes, only darkness. He was like Andy and all the greats who came before him: Bundy, Fish, Dahmer, Gacy…

The boy could be one of the best, but he would never see his true potential; Andy was going to kill him. Even if he never made it out of the woods from the wound in his chest, he'd take another soul with him to the hell that surely awaited him on the other side of life.

Andy's chest hurt, but he had a renewed vigor at the thought of getting another kill. Slowly, so as not to aggravate his injury, he went to work on the rope.

***

The boys stood at the crossroads that would send them in different directions towards their houses. They stopped their bikes with the front tires facing in, so they were like spokes.

"I've been thinking about it," JJ began, "and I think we wait to tell our parents until the morning."

Nick and Matt looked at him like he had lobsters coming out of his ears.

"Why? We should tell them now so the cops can go get him and we can get paid," Matt said.

Nick nodded in agreement. "Yeah, JJ, I'm with Matt. That guy is a killer, man. He needs to be in a cage or dead."

"Absolutely," JJ said. "But he's not going anywhere soon, right?" He was looking at Nick. "What kind of wound did you say he had?"

"A sucking chest wound. His lung is probably completely collapsed, so he's only running on one right now. Plus, it probably hurts like hell."

"Right, so he's not going to spring up and go running out of the woods. He's probably lucky to be alive as it is. If we tell our parents tonight, they might not even believe us. And if they do and call the cops, *they* might not believe us. I'm sure they're getting tons of tips about this guy, and running down a lead at night, in the middle of the woods, probably isn't something they're going to do. And I don't know about you two, but I certainly don't want to go hiking through the woods, in the dark, trying to show them where a serial killer is." JJ looked at each of them, letting the logic of his words sink in.

"Yeah, I think JJ is right," Nick said.

Matt nodded, going with the flow. "Okay. I think you have a point. I sure as shit don't want to go out tonight looking for him, even with the cops. Plus, I want to see if I can beat *Super Mario 64* tonight."

"Good. So tomorrow, we tell our parents, and they can call the cops. Then we'll all get paid," JJ said with a smile.

"Hell yeah," Nick said.

"Sounds good to me."

The first streetlight came to life, signaling to the boys their night was at an end.

They all headed towards home.

JJ pedaled hard, pumping his legs with a burning fury. His mind raced faster than the two wheels beneath him. He was trying to remember where his dad's flashlight was. His night was far from over.

***

Andy's chest was on fire. The pressure on his shoulders didn't help the matter. With his hands tied behind his back, the tension on the wound seemed to increase. Luckily, the kid who tied the knot was no boy scout.

As soon as the boys were out of earshot, Andy went to work on the knot. It wasn't tight, but enough of a hindrance, especially in his state, to give him a hard time. The sun was dipping into the trees, and he knew another cold night awaited him. But there was something else in his mind, a glimmer he held onto.

Hope.

It was a look he'd seen many times on the faces of his victims, their last plea, hoping to touch a piece of his sympathy, which didn't exist. And there he was, hoping for a miracle.

The one boy—JJ—had it in him. He had the same darkness Andy possessed, an evil inside which made him want to hurt. He was still young, but

Andy knew the boy had already acted on his urges; the looks on the faces of the other two were proof enough. *Fear.* They had fear in their eyes when they looked at him.

Sweat soaked Andy's shirt as he worked against the knot. The blood on his chest had clotted, but he worried about ripping the wound back open. Over the day, his breathing had improved a little, but staying in the woods was a death sentence. If he could find his way out, he might have a chance. By that time, his face would be all over every news outlet, so going to the hospital was out of the question.

While he could survive with one lung, Andy didn't think the damaged one was punctured as badly as he first thought. Even though his breathing hadn't much improved, he knew he could survive the injury if he didn't die of exposure.

The rope loosened and feeling returned to his hands.

"Come on, you motherfucker," he growled.

The sun dipped, and brown light filled the woods. He couldn't see much that wasn't directly in front of him.

Pain coursed through his arms, but the rope moved more and more, until he slipped his wrists from it. Andy shuddered as his arms came free. He put them up to his face and blew on his chilly hands. More light bled from the forest, and with it, any semblance of warmth.

Slowly, he stood. Pain filled his chest, but his breathing was slightly better. He didn't know if that was from the adrenaline rushing through his bloodstream or his body healing, but he would take it.

The boys had a campsite nearby. During the first day of his escape from the law, and subsequent injury, he hadn't noticed the rudimentary set up. After the boys came crashing through the trees like a herd of elephants, it was quite obvious where they were. Before they'd seen him, Andy smelled smoke and saw their little blaze. Why they wanted a fire on a warm day was beside him, but he was little once. Young boys did strange things.

Slowly, in the waning light, Andy trekked into the camp. The boys left nothing behind, but never extinguished the fire before leaving, a terrible habit, but it might save the wounded man's life. The flames were long gone, but the embers remained warm to the touch. Andy wasn't much concerned with the charred wood, but with the rocks circling the pit.

River stones held heat better than wood. Andy picked one up the size of a grapefruit. It was hot, just enough to almost be unbearable, but to him, it felt like a new lease on life. Gently, he pressed the stone to his chest. His wound burned from within, but the heat from the rock gave him a boost of strength.

Night had fallen. The woods were dark, except for the moonlight fighting its way through the treetops. Night creatures were coming out to feed and fuck, but something else was moving through the gloom.

Andy looked in the direction the boys had come and gone. Someone was moving toward him, but not with the pace of recklessness. They were taking their time, but still seemed to crack and break every branch along the path. The sound stopped and a flashlight lit up the area. For a second, Andy's heart sank, thinking the cops had finally caught up to him. But if it were the pigs, they wouldn't be traveling alone, and they certainly wouldn't be quiet. He knew who it was and what he wanted to do.

After impaling himself on the branch, Andy thought he might never get the chance to feel the slow ebb of life drift away from a child again. But like almost everything in his life, Andy found a way.

With the warm rock pressed against his chest, he slowly made his way back to the tree. He had a trap to set.

***

"Fuck," JJ said. A branch whipped his face. He swatted it away, continuing his crawl through the dark woods.

It was a path he'd walked hundreds of times, but never in the dark, and never in search of a killer. A few times he thought he was lost. Even using the flashlight didn't always help. Shadows played with his sense of direction and focus. A deeply rooted fear of the dark gripped his heart, but still, he pushed on. He was determined.

He was getting closer to the campsite, and thus, closer to Andy Lakken, child killer. JJ was scared and excited to find the murderer. To be one-on-one with a man who'd taken human life was on another level for JJ. It was dangerous and reckless, but it was a once-in-a-lifetime opportunity. If the man wasn't so badly wounded, JJ didn't know if he would've had the courage to make the hike, especially alone.

He turned the light on for just a moment, confirming where he was along the trail. JJ turned it off, giving his eyes a second to readjust before setting off again, the smile on his face hidden in the darkness.

***

Andy was against the tree again. He would wait for the last possible moment before putting his hands behind his back, feigning being tied up. His fingers were full of strength. The pain in his chest was burning from his jaunt to the campsite and back, but it was worth it. He did his best to slow his breathing, allowing his good lung to provide oxygen. Andy would need the strength.

The flashlight was on again, and much closer. So close, he could see the outline of the boy. He was alone.

"Ah, you've come back," Andy said as JJ entered the small clearing where he'd made his home over the last day or so. He slipped his hands behind his back.

JJ didn't talk, just walked closer to Andy. He stopped in front of the wounded man with the flashlight pointed in his face.

It was hard for Andy not to pull his unsecured hands from behind him to block the offensive beam. JJ was smarter than he thought, using a simple ploy to see whether or not Andy was still tied up.

Clever boy.

"That's pretty annoying," Andy said, turning his head away from the beam.

JJ lowered the light from Andy's eyes, aiming it at his chest.

"Much better." With his vision returning, Andy did a quick sweep of the boy's belt line. He didn't see the big knife he was carrying earlier in the day, but that didn't mean it wasn't tucked away in the boy's backpack.

JJ unshouldered his pack and set it on the ground. "Why?"

Andy turned his head in question. "I'm sorry? Why what?"

JJ licked his lips, but the flashlight didn't waver. It was still pointed at Andy's chest.

He didn't know if JJ could tell the sucking chest wound was doing better or not. Andy forced a cough to show he was still hurt.

"Why do you kill?"

Andy grinned. "Why do you?"

JJ looked shocked, at least at first. "I-I don't."

"Oh, come on. Yes, you do. Maybe you haven't taken the life of a person yet, but you've killed. You've maimed and tortured. I know you've spent a sleepless night wondering why it felt so good to set a cat on fire or to shove pins into a trapped mouse, why you convinced the other two to do it with you. You want to feel normal, like what *we* are is something normal." Andy leaned a little closer. "We're not ordinary, JJ." He scrunched up his face. "JJ? I assume that's not your real name, is it? A nickname of sorts."

JJ nodded. "Yeah, it's just what everyone calls me. I don't particularly like my first name, even though Dad told me it was one of my heroic ancestor's names."

"And, pray tell, what is this name you don't like?"

JJ rolled his eyes as only a teenage boy could. "Jasper. Jasper Jenkins."

Andy nodded. "That's a good name, Jasper. I like it. It has a pleasant tone to it. I can see it now, in years to come when you're in bloom, reigning terror, 'Man at large: Serial killer Jasper Jenkins is on the loose again, killing at will.' See, it has a great sound to it."

He lowered his voice just a decibel or two. Talking the boy up was working. It was something Andy had done time and time again—luring his victims with the smoothness of his voice, bringing them closer into his snare before springing the trap that would end their lives.

Andy's fingers burned with anticipation as he looked at the budding Adam's apple protruding from Jasper's neck. It was the perfect size for his thumbs. If he was going to die in those woods, or be captured, he needed one last soul to usher him into the afterlife.

Jasper squatted on his haunches and set the flashlight on the ground. He dug through the bag and pulled out a canteen.

Andy wanted to reach out and grab it with both hands, upending it all over him, drinking until he was full to bursting. But patience had gotten him that far, and he knew the boy would have to get closer so he could drink. When Jasper's body was headed toward room temperature, then he would drink more.

"If I help you, will you help me?" Jasper asked. He leaned in with the canteen in his left hand.

The mouth of the bottle moved toward Andy's parched lips. He let the cool water run down his dry throat. It tasted faintly of plastic, but it was ambrosia. He felt physical pain when Jasper pulled the bottle away.

"Help you with what?"

Jasper looked him in the eyes. "Killing. I know what I am, but I'm scared."

Andy chuckled. "Of course you're scared. It's fucking scary. But do you want to know why it's so scary? Because it's so much fucking fun. To watch the life fade from their eyes, knowing you're the last thing they'll ever see before drifting away into nothing, it's better than anything." He had him; Jasper's eyes were wide, like he was Mickey Mouse.

The boy unconsciously inched closer, just enough so Andy knew he was in range. His throat waited for him, called him. He could already hear and feel the soft cartilage of the boy's windpipe crushing under his thumbs.

"I just want my first one to be special, something I'll remember forever," Jasper said.

Andy nodded. His shoulders twitched as he prepared to attack. "Oh, you'll remember them all. Each one is special. Each face will be tattooed upon your brain. You'll see them in your dreams, sometimes even awake. I'll never forget them, especially this one."

The calm persona Andy had been projecting was gone. His pale face contorted into a mask of rage and hatred, a mixture of pleasure and pain, as he lunged forward. The surprised look on Jasper's face was heavenly as his hands wrapped around the boy's neck.

The canteen fell and Jasper's hands went to Andy's, but the kid didn't have the strength of a man, and never would.

Andy gritted his teeth and squeezed.

***

JJ was dying. He knew it was a bad idea, yet he'd still made the walk. He sought out this man—this monster—and asked for his help. He wasn't sure what he expected. Part of him thought this was for the better: die before he became a killer like the man in front of him. But no, Jasper knew the real reason he made the journey into the woods. Andy was going to be his first kill. Tied up, wounded, and a person deserving of death—it was a simple decision. He would talk with the serial killer until he'd worked up the nerve to draw the blade hidden behind his back. But, it seemed Andy had other plans.

JJ was blacking out and pulling at the man's hands wasn't working. It was difficult, but he released his grasp and reached behind his back. The blade glimmered in the flashlight's beam, and for just a second, JJ saw Andy's gaze flicker to the knife. The fear in his eyes, and the realization he was about to die, were the greatest things JJ had ever seen. Even with his consciousness on the fringes, he smiled.

The blade entered just above Andy's belly button at an upward angle. Steel deflated his good lung and the strength of his grasp wavered.

JJ pulled the blade back and stabbed again. Soft meat and organs hardly slowed it down. Again, he stabbed. Warm gore wet the edge of the blade and his hand.

Andy's grasp faltered and went slack.

JJ took a deep breath and stood. His heart was racing and his throat was on fire, but he was alive. He was warm with the dump of adrenaline and the wetness of his victim's blood.

Andy's hands were on his ruined gut trying to stem the flow of his lifeblood. Bile, shit, and bits of ruined organs peeked from the slices in his body.

JJ looked at the dying man like a painter admires his art. "This was my plan the entire time, but I'm guessing you knew that," JJ said. He rubbed his injured neck. "It would've been better if you didn't strangle me, but I guess I'll have to come up with a cover story."

Andy was gasping for air. Blood bubbled up from his mouth and his skin was ashen. A tear ran down his face.

JJ looked at the knife, feeling the power of it coursing through his body. "You were right. This is something I'll never forget. The first of many."

In the darkness of the trees, under the watchful gaze of the night creatures, JJ killed. He killed with a smile on his face.

Andy Lakken was found days later, ripped apart by coyotes and other scavengers.

Jasper didn't know if the autopsy revealed the fact he was stabbed to death, but if it did, it was never made public.

As for the marks on his neck, his parents hardly cared. They took his excuse that he was wrestling with Nick and Matt at face value and didn't mention it again.

JJ never told Nick and Matt, or uttered another word about Andy Lakken, but they knew. The next day, he easily convinced them to not report what they found, that Andy would get off easy in the courts, and probably get life in prison and not the death penalty. Leaving him in the woods, tied up for the coyotes to get him, was the justice he deserved. Jasper knew they didn't like that idea, but there was a look of fear in their eyes the next day. He changed, and they knew it; it was like a mother knowing the day her daughter loses her virginity. There was just something about the way they moved, or smelled, or talked. It wasn't something that could be explained, but it was known.

20 years later

Her name was Becca. She'd been too trusting of him, with her little girl grin and the streamers on her bike.

It was easy for JJ, who now went by Jasper. It only took a practiced smile and feigned interest in the girl's bicycle stunts; Becca loved showing off on her bike.

Jasper's car bounced down the road with Becca bound and gagged in the trunk. He'd killed many since the day in the woods, but he'd never forget his first.

Jasper Jenkins was a scourge to the Northeast, killing up and down the coast, similar to the man he considered a mentor. It was a macabre passing of the torch, so to speak.

The car hit a bump and Becca squealed through her gag.

Jasper laughed, knowing what fun he was going to have with her. He drove further, winding through a wooded road. There was a cabin awaiting them, and he couldn't wait to get there.

FAIR FOOD

The street fair smelled like body odor and shitty food. Each smell could've been easily interchanged with the other, but to Steven Cosgrove, it was Heaven on Earth.

Steve walked up to yet another food vendor, gazing at the treats laid out in front of him.

"Steven Phillip Cosgrove, if you eat any more shit, you're going to explode," Martha told her husband.

If either of them looked like they were on the verge of explosion, it was her. Martha stood at just over five feet, but was almost as round. Her dyed-red hair had lost some of its luster and a few grays were peeking through. She had teeth that looked remotely like a dolphin's that hadn't seen a dentist in years.

Steven couldn't have been more opposite. He was tall and slender, but had a voracious appetite. He ate it all, including his wife's pussy, when she asked. He had a little belly, but the only reason it stuck out was because of the absolute lack of muscle mass. The amount of times he'd been checked for tapeworms was in the double digits. Every doctor told him the same thing: he had a high metabolism people would kill for.

Martha grabbed Steven's hand with her sweaty one. "Come on," she said, tugging on him. "I want to look at the wind chimes." Martha gave another pull, this time putting a little weight into it.

Steven couldn't fight his wife any more than he could fight a boulder rolling downhill. He looked at the food left behind, and felt a grumble in his stomach. It could've been from the fried crap he'd eaten over the last hour, but it felt like hunger again.

They waded into the sea of people, Martha like a plow against the wave of flesh. She glanced back at her husband with a look of lust on her sweaty face.

"If you're a good boy, I'll let you eat something else later," she said, winking, the fat folds around her eye doubling in creases.

They walked and Martha shopped, loading up her husband with bags full of cheap trinkets and shit. And still, they didn't stop at any more food vendors.

Steven felt like a child being towed around with his mother. He looked at all the delicious treats they moved by, each one calling to his rumbling stomach.

Martha looked at him as the growl subsided.

"Was that your stomach?" she asked, slowing her pace. The crowd moved around them, most with grumbles, with a couple of 'fat bitch' comments thrown in.

Steve rubbed his gut, which was begging for something to eat. Anything to eat.

"Yeah, I've been trying to tell you, I'm fucking starving."

Martha threw up her hands in frustration. "I don't know where you put it." She looked him up and down, as if she'd never seen him before.

Steve smiled. “Fast metabolism.” It looked like he was going to get something else to eat, after all. Steve spun, looking. Something exotic caught his nose. It was almost calling to him, pulling him past the fried cookies and candy. It wafted between the cheap cheesesteaks and pulled pork. No, this was something different, something he hadn’t gorged himself on. He scanned, trying to use his nose like a cartoon character and finally, he saw it.

The small food cart was tucked away behind another vendor selling a bit of everything.

“There,” he pointed to the little cart.

Martha put a hand over her eyes and looked. “Where?”

“Right there,” Steven said, pointing past the bigger stand.

Martha saw the cart and turned to her husband. “Out of all the great food, you want that little, dinky-shit cart?”

“Yup,” he said with a smile, handing over all the bags she’d accumulated over the day. Steve was already walking towards it, his mind made up.

A man stood at the cart, a smile plastered on his face.

“What are you selling, my good man?” Steven asked. The heavenly aroma wafting up was almost too much for him. He didn’t care what the man was selling, he needed it.

The man didn’t say a word, just kept smiling.

Steven figured it was some kind of ethnic food, possibly Middle Eastern by the appearance of the man, but he wasn't too worldly. The vendor probably didn't speak English, which was why the tourism board stuck him in the back.

Well, Steven didn't stand for that shit. If this man was trying to make a living, Steven was going to support the hell out of him. He pulled $20 from his wallet and held it out.

"I'll take however many I can get for this."

The man kept smiling, but money always talked. He gave Steven a nod and opened the top of the cart.

Steam and the smell of meaty heaven wafted out of the opening. The vendor reached in and pulled out a bouquet of meat on a stick.

Steven was nearly drooling and didn't even notice Martha at his back. He handed the man the money and took the bundle of meat. It looked like pork, but he didn't know.

"Thank you," Steven said, and gave the man a slight bow.

The man stuffed the money into his pocket and continued smiling.

His face must get tired from that, Steven thought.

"Steven, you can't be serious?" Martha asked, as they walked away from the cart. The smell of the meat appeared to be making her nauseous.

Steven took a bite gingerly, to not burn himself. Juices and flavors he never experienced flooded his mouth. Burned tongue be damned. Steven inhaled the first meat stick in seconds.

"Oh, I'm serious alright," he said back with a smile. His lips were coated in grease. "I'm so serious." He threw the stick out and chomped into number two.

Martha huffed, but knew it was a losing battle. Her hubby liked to eat.

"Fine, but if you're up all night, sitting on the pot, don't say I didn't warn you."

Steve gave her a thumbs up; his mouth was too full to speak. He followed his wife to yet another table of knick-knacks she didn't need.

The meat was delicious, and within their little walk to look at trinkets and baubles, he'd eaten all of them.

Martha looked at him, disgusted, as Steven let out a belch. Even a few people, especially those that were close, sneered at him as well.

"Ugh," Martha groaned, "you're disgusting." She turned from her husband and continued to examine her next purchase.

***

Martha handed Steven yet another bag. This one contained what was essentially a painted yardstick that measured snow. Except it cost $15, and not $3, like in the hardware store.

Steven adjusted the bags, trying to find a comfortable way to hold them. His stomach rumbled and he realized he had stuffed no fair food in his mouth since that meat-on-a-stick. His mouth watered at the thought of that rich, meaty goodness. They had to walk past the cart on the way to the parking lot, so why not grab a few for the road?

"What are you looking for?" Martha asked, fanning herself with a brochure. Her skin was pink and glistening, giving her a swine-like appearance.

Steven scanned. It was much easier now since the fair was ending shortly. Some vendors were trying to make last-minute sales, and others were already packing up. He hoped his meat-on-a-stick guy was still there. Hell, maybe he could get a deal and buy the rest of his stock. He'd have snacks for a few days.

"I'm trying to find that meat cart again." Steven's eyes were scanning. Martha was ready to go home, and a detour would ruffle her feathers. Not that he really cared, but he didn't want to hear her bitch. She was already hot and tired, plus her feet hurt. He knew what that meant; in addition to going down on her, he'd be rubbing her swollen feet and cankles.

"Really?" she asked, as if her excess shopping was any different from his excess eating.

Steven didn't justify that with a response, he was in search mode. He spotted the bigger stands, the ones that concealed the tiny food cart. His heart raced like a kid on Christmas.

"There," he almost shouted, pointing to the bigger stands. At a fast walk, Steven pushed through the light crowd. He used his wife's bags to shuffle people out of his way until he reached his destination.

Steven's stomach sank when he saw a blank spot where the cart was. Gone. He didn't even get a business card from the vendor.

Martha came up behind him, huffing, sounding like a steam engine.

"Gone?" she asked the obvious. "Well, you didn't need it anyway." As if she was one to talk about weight. "Let's get going," she said, tapping him on the shoulder. "I need a soak. My feet are killing me." She made eye contact with him, making sure he understood what was going to happen later.

Steven was upset about the food but plastered on a smile.

"Okay, come on," he said, letting his wife guide him to the parking lot.

***

The rest of the night was uneventful. Steven and Martha went home, unloaded the bags, and cleaned up. Steven was right; his wife wanted oral, which he performed like a champion, and a foot rub. His husbandly skills must've been good because she gave him a quick hand job afterward. It was rough and hurt a little, but it was better than nothing.

Steven laid in bed, listening to the low snores of Martha. She was out like a light, but he couldn't seem to get comfortable. His stomach was rumbling and not in a hungry way. There was no chance he would've told his wife; he didn't want to hear her shit about eating all of that food.

Steven pushed back the blankets and walked into the master bathroom. The medicine cabinet was full of Martha's pills, mainly for her cholesterol and blood pressure. He scanned, and looked for a bottle of antacids, or something to calm his stomach. Then it rumbled again, and this was not a heartburn rumble.

Steven pulled down his pajama pants and jumped on the toilet. At first, nothing happened and then he erupted. Hot, loose shit poured from him in a quick burst, but then it was over. No more bubble-guts or cramping.

"Oh, fuck," he said, mumbling as he grabbed the toilet paper. The relief was almost as good as the handy he got earlier. He wiped, stood up, and flushed.

If he'd taken a second to look in the toilet, he would've seen his mushy shit wriggling with tiny, black bodies.

***

Steven sat at his desk, his fingers flying over the keyboard. Data entry wasn't the most glamorous job, but it paid the bills. The office was usually an ice box, but that day Steven was feeling a bit warm. He looked at the small clock hanging on his cubicle wall and realized it was only 11 am. He still had six hours until the end of the day.

Steven loosened his tie, noticing the dampness of his collar. He felt fine that morning, especially after that disgusting shit he'd taken in the middle of the night. His stomach cramped and rolled; he knew another one was coming.

Steven would rarely shit at work if he could avoid it. There was nothing like your own bowl at home. He didn't think the shit he had brewing was going to last another six hours.

With just a few more clicks, he was done with the current entry. He pushed himself away from his desk, and stood up. The pressure in his bowels doubled, and he clenched his ass tight as a little fart slipped out. He hoped it was only gas.

Gingerly, he made his way to the bathroom. No one else was in there, which was a blessing; he was about to blow the place up.

Steven opened a stall and another urge twisted in his guts. Frantically, he pulled at his belt and cheap suit pants. He hit the bowl and unleashed.

The foul, putrid odor of hot shit filled the bathroom. He stood, crouching over the bowl, and flushed. He didn't need anyone else getting a whiff of that. After another minute or two, Steven felt relief.

"Damn." He put his sweaty face in his hands. "Maybe Martha was right." He usually had an iron stomach, but something at the fair fucked him up good.

Steven unrolled a healthy amount of cheap toilet paper.

"Ow, what the fuck?" he muttered. His ass was suddenly burning, like he'd been stung by a bee. Gently, he wiped and looked at the toilet paper.

Shit. Shit and blood streaked the 2-ply, but there was something else. Something tiny burrowed in the lump of bloody stool. It was a little bug. Steven put the lump of shit closer to his face and realized it looked like a tiny centipede, but instead of the normal reddish coloring, it was black.

He threw the clump of tissue into the bowl and grabbed another wad. This wipe came back with less shit and no blood. Steven stared at the toilet paper.

Did I just fucking imagine that? He didn't think he did, but there was absolutely no blood and no sign of any more creepy crawlies.

The door to the bathroom banged open, and Steven almost dropped the toilet paper. He threw it in the toilet, wiped until he was satisfied, and waited. Even though he did a courtesy flush, the stench of his shit was still lingering. Once he was alone, he buttoned up and left.

The rest of the day he sat at his desk without a rumble in his guts. But, no matter what, he couldn't help but think about the centipede on the toilet paper...and of course, the blood.

***

Steven slid into bed next to his wife, who was scrolling through her phone aimlessly. He was tired, and even though it wasn't too late, he was ready to sleep.

"Good night," he kissed Martha on the cheek, which she offered, but didn't take her eyes from her phone.

"Night," she said back, laughing at a meme.

Steven rolled over and turned off his light. Within minutes, he was asleep, but he wouldn't be for very long.

***

Steven awoke in a panic. The room was dark, but the glow of his alarm clock showed it was just after midnight. He was soaked in sweat and for a moment he thought he'd pissed himself. A cramp ripped through his guts, and he felt like he was going to puke.

Steven threw the covers off, not caring if he woke Martha, and ran into the bathroom.

He flipped on the lights, not giving his eyes time to adjust, and looked into the mirror. He looked like shit: pale, sweating, and with heavy bags under his eyes.

Steven, for all the food he'd ever eaten, never had food poisoning, but he was pretty damn sure that had changed.

A pressure was building behind his eye. It wasn't quite a headache, but it sure as hell hurt.

"Fuck," he mumbled, putting a clammy hand to his temple. The pain felt like a writhing, creeping pressure. Then it hit him. Something was behind his eye.

Steven leaned over the sink and pried his eyelid open. His tear duct quivered, and the pain was becoming next to unbearable. He pushed his face closer to the mirror until his breath fogged it up. He stared at his tear duct, or rather next to it. A pair of tiny antennas poked out of his flesh.

Steven gasped and pushed away from the mirror. He didn't want to believe what he'd just seen. It couldn't be real; he must still be dreaming. Slowly, and on bated breath, he moved back to the mirror.

The antennas were out, along with the fat head of the centipede. The black body was still struggling through, but the head, with the wide mandibles, was free.

Tiny legs dug into the slick surface of his eye, each one a separate sting, as the bug worked its way out of his flesh.

Steven, ever so gently, reached to pluck the little intruder from his burning eye. He realized he hadn't blinked and the searing pain was getting to him. His fingers closed on the wriggling body, finding purchase.

Then it bit.

The serrated jaws ripped into the orb, causing white to turn red.

"Ah!" he screamed, as he ripped it from his eye. The pain was electric and once the centipede was free, he blinked. Blood and tears flowed, weeping down his cheek.

Steven's stomach felt like it was flipping, and he knew he was going to puke. He didn't know if it was from the pain of his bloody eye, or the nausea he felt in bed, but whatever it was, it was winning.

He grabbed the side of the sink and unleashed.

A torrent of vomit, mostly consisting of the pizza and ice cream he'd had for dinner, sprayed into the sink. It splashed against the wall, speckling the toothbrush cups. The remnants of his meal weren't the only thing in his vomit. Small, black centipedes crawled from the quagmire of filth.

He watched them squirm with his one good eye; the other was blurry and throbbing. Steven's stomach clenched again, feeling like he'd eaten a bag of nails. This time it was coming from the other end. He fumbled with his pajama bottoms, lumbering towards the toilet.

"Fuck, fuck, fuck," he said. Steven waddled, clenching his ass cheeks shut, but it was no use. His foot found a slimy chunk of half-digested pizza and he slipped. Steven didn't fall, but the concentration he was using to not shit his pants faltered.

A wet fart ripped from his ass. To Steven, it felt endless. Hot, chunky shit ran down his legs, coating his pajamas and feet.

Steven's legs were weak. He felt like he was on the verge of passing out and leaned against the wall. Slowly, he slid down, not caring about the squishy shit in his pants. The cramps had subsided and he was grateful. At least for the moment.

"Ow, what the fuck?" A sharp pinch in his thigh snapped him back to reality. "Fuck." Another pinch, this one felt like a bee sting and was on his other leg. Steven pulled his pants down, exposing his feces-covered groin and legs, and almost fainted.

The centipedes, the same ones he'd shit and puked out, covered his lower body.

"Oh, shit." He swatted at the bugs. They were no longer the little, tiny things he'd seen the day before, but some were much larger. One was the size of his thumb. The jaws on it were wide and sharp and made for cutting through flesh.

Steven could feel the legs tickling him and he brushed at it, hoping to swat it off. The bug bit, but this wasn't a pinch or a bee sting.

"Fuck!" he screamed, watching the carnivorous little thing take a chunk of him. Within moments the flesh was devoured, and the bug grew.

Steven pulled at the centipede, hoping to get it before it bit again.

"Cocksucker!" he groaned, feeling the sting of more tiny jaws eating him.

"Steven?" Martha banged on the bathroom door. "Steven, honey, are you okay?" She tried the knob, but he had locked it. "Steven, open the door." She shook the door on its frame, but it wouldn't budge. "I heard you scream. Please let me in." Her voice wavered, but still the door remained closed.

"No," he groaned, a new burning forming in his guts. "Don't come in here." He burped, more vomit rising from his stomach. Except this wasn't puke, but pure bugs.

A black wave of slick centipedes showered his chest. They wasted no time setting about their feast.

Steven pulled them off, trying to throw them into the toilet or sink, but there were too many.

Blood coated his body, along with puke and shit.

"Steven, I'm going to get the key," Martha shrieked. She nearly shook the house as she ran downstairs.

Steven felt the sting of hundreds of jaws on his chest, and ripped his shirt off. His chest hair was matted with a writhing mass of blood and ever-growing black centipedes. He grabbed handfuls of bugs, ripping them from his body. They came off in clumps, taking ragged strips of flesh with them.

His legs were just as bad. The bugs had grown and with each bite they took more and more of him.

Steven's hands were covered in welts and bites. Each time he tried to swat some away, they'd grab at his skin, stinging him mercilessly.

Nausea and an earth-shattering pain wrenched his stomach. He didn't feel like he was going to puke or shit, but the pressure was unbearable. It was so bad that it overshadowed the pain of the biting. Steven looked at his stomach in horror.

His lower abdomen, just before his pubic hair, bulged. He stared and, for a moment, the rest of the centipedes stopped biting. It was as if they were looking, too. The lump in his gut moved, the skin stretching. The bulge moved further south, pressing into his bladder. Steven pissed uncontrollably as the creature writhed. Frantically, he pulled his urine-soaked underwear off.

His pubic hair formed a mound, as the lump moved further. And then, it stopped.

Steven was sweating. Each drop burned his tormented flesh, but the centipedes on his body had stopped attacking him. Even their legs were still. The only movement was from their twitching antennas.

"Ah!" Steven screamed. The lump began to thrash and bite from inside. Red-tinted piss spurted from his flaccid penis, before turning into pure blood. It was as if his scream was a starter pistol, giving the rest of the bugs permission to continue their feast. Thousands of jaws ripped into him again, seeking bloody holes and new meat.

Steven reached for his crotch as a pair of black mandibles the size of fingers tore through skin and hair.

The giant centipede squeezed through like an unholy birth. Blood oozed from the destroyed flesh and the centipede wore Steven's deflated bladder like a macabre shroud. Thick legs sprouted from the wound, pulling the hellish bug from Steven's gut.

The clicking jaws were looking for the next piece of flesh and found it.

In one bite, the centipede tore Steven's cock from his body. Blood spurted as his member was ripped free and eaten by the creature.

"Steven, I'm here," Martha shrieked. She rattled at the door, trying to get the key into the lock. "I'm coming!"

Steven was fading. The pain was gone, replaced by numbness. He only felt little tugs here and there. The massive centipede was eating his testicles, but he didn't care anymore. The edges of his vision were fading, like he was drifting off to sleep. In a way, he was. In the back of his mind, he could hear Martha yelling. Part of him could decipher what she was saying, but he couldn't warn her.

He closed his eyes, knowing he'd soon be gone. The crunching and chewing continued, but it sounded far off in the distance. His battered nerves felt a cool breeze as the door flew open.

The crunching and chewing were joined by another sound.

Screaming.

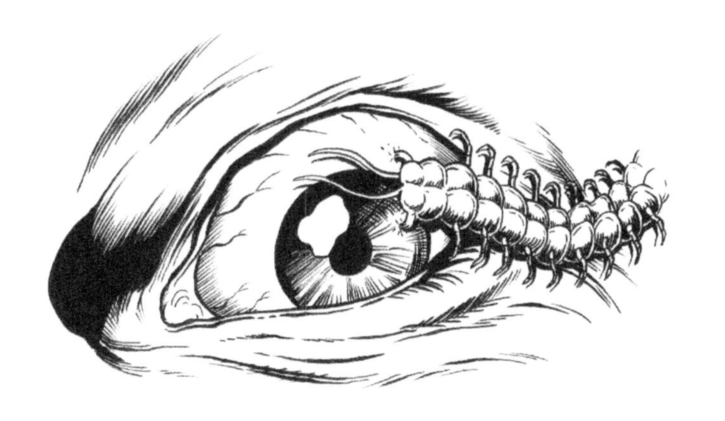

GOING SOUTH

Going south.

That was the answer most people received when they asked, “So, what are you going to do when you retire?”

New York was a great state to make a lot of money, and pay a lot of taxes, but it was far from ideal when it came to retirement. So, many people took their hard-earned retirement and headed south. It was almost always decent weather, the people were friendly, and everything was cheap. It was as if they were stuck in the 1980s.

“Are you ready?” Larry asked Helen as he buckled his seatbelt and looked at his wife.

She smiled, light crow’s feet at her eyes. “Do I have a choice?” She adjusted her belt, getting it off her neck.

Larry checked the rearview mirror. It was the last time he would ever see his New York driveway again. “Nope.” He leaned over, kissed her, and put the car in reverse.

Their house looked weird without any curtains, but those were in the moving truck, which was already going south. The *SOLD* sign planted in the front yard swung in the breeze.

Larry and Helen took off, ready to start their lives as retirees.

Helen taught for just under 40 years, retiring last January.

Larry did 30 years with the county as a civil engineer. He retired 5 years before Helen, and had been waiting to leave New York since. His pension was great, but the state bled him dry.

Finally, the day had arrived. He loved Tennessee. The people, the land, the atmosphere, and of course, the low taxes. When Helen was approaching retirement, Larry started looking at houses in the Volunteer State. He and Helen would go down for a week or two and house hunt.

Before long, they found their dream house. It was a 2000-square-foot raised ranch, only 5 years old, sitting on 5 acres, with a pond. Larry laughed at the price. That house in his NY neighborhood would've been double and the yearly taxes were what he paid in a month up north.

They had been driving for 10 hours and were finally entering Tennessee. Night had fallen and the oncoming headlights were bothering Larry's eyes.

"Hel, watch for the exit. Let me know when it's coming up. I don't want to take my eyes off the road," he said, hunkering down over the steering wheel.

"Gladly," she replied. "Your driving is questionable during the day."

"Ah, you're no better. Now, keep an eye out for the exit. This one always sneaks up on me." Larry was hunched over the wheel, his old eyes looking for the off ramp. "What did that say?" he asked his wife as the green sign went by in a blur.

"I'm not sure, I think it was exit 104," she said, craning her neck to look back at the sign.

"Fuck," he muttered. Another sign was approaching. "Next exit 35 miles," he read. "Goddammit," he smacked the steering wheel. "I hate that fucking exit."

Helen sipped from her water to keep from chuckling. Larry was so cute when he was angry, which he rarely was. She didn't want to drink too much; Larry hated stopping for bathroom breaks. He seemed like he was always trying to beat his time with every trip down.

"Just make a U-turn and head back," she said.

Larry thought about it. He really didn't want to get a ticket, but he desperately wanted to get to the house. The movers were already there and were unloading. If they didn't get there soon, the movers would just drop everything in the living room, leaving them to lug it all around the house.

He didn't see any cop cars, and quickly made a U-turn. He accelerated, and when he didn't see any flashing lights behind him, he relaxed. "Okay, let's keep a look out for that damn exit," he said, driving slowly in the right lane.

The exit approached. He breathed a sigh of relief as he took the sweeping road off the highway. He got to the end of the ramp and put on his right blinker just before he noticed the *ROAD CLOSED* signs.

"Shit. Not a great start to retirement, Hel," he said, turning left.

"We should've bought a GPS."

He waved her off. Larry didn't like technology. He always said his GPS was a good old map, which he was looking around for. "Helen, where's my map?"

"I'm not sure, but can you keep your eyes on the road?"

The car was drifting over the fog line.

Larry swerved back into his lane.

A road sign showed a gas station 2 miles away.

"I'm going to go to the gas station and check the map." The gas gauge was over half. "Might as well fill up, too," he said.

"Good, because I kind of have to pee." Helen squirmed in her seat.

The yellow lights buzzed above the gas pumps as Larry stopped in front of a pump and got out to fill the tank.

Helen went inside the store and when Larry finished, he followed.

The store was nearly empty. The clerk, a mid-30s guy with greasy hair, stood behind the counter reading a book. Two men and a woman were figuring out if they had enough cash for a 30 pack of beer or if they'd have to settle for an 18 pack.

Larry bought a large coffee—black—and a bag of beef jerky. He took his map from his jacket pocket and sat at a table. He spread it out, putting on his glasses so he could make out the tiny lines.

Helen slid in across from him. "So, where do we need to go?" she asked, sipping her coffee.

Larry could barely see; his vision was getting worse. "I'm not sure, but I think I have an idea."

"Where y'all going?"

Larry looked to his left; the beer trio was standing at their table.

He took his glasses off. "Headed to Maryville, but the road closure kind of has us in a bind. We need to pick up County Route 41, but this map is giving me issues."

"Nah, you don't need no map. We're heading to a friend's house in Maryville. You can just follow us," he smiled at them.

Larry hated stereotypes, but this group fit the bill. The guy doing the talking stood average height. He had on dirty blue jeans, a multi tool on his belt, and a knife in his pocket. He wore a sleeveless plaid shirt, which was open, revealing a white tank top underneath. His ensemble was completed with a confederate flag adorned hat and patchy beard.

The other guy he was with was similar in height, but weighed a solid 300 lbs. He was clean shaven, head and face. His meaty arms were covered in shitty tattoos. He wore a tank top and camo shorts. A hunting knife hung from his belt, and there was a circular tin of tobacco in his front pocket.

The girl was semi-normal. She was as skinny as a rail. Her hair was messy and the color of swamp water. Acne scars dimpled her face and her cheeks were sunken. Her shorts were loose on her thighs, and she wore no bra, not that she had any breasts to support.

Larry had never seen an actual meth head, but he figured this girl was what they would look like. He glanced at Helen, who was nervously smiling. He didn't like the trio, but they needed to get to the house, and this group could help them, hopefully.

"Lead the way," said Larry, standing up.

The talker extended his hand. "Name's Gunner." He pointed to the fat one. "That's Clint," and then the girl, "and Nancy."

Larry took his hand. "Larry. Nice to meet you," he nodded to the other two, "and thanks again."

"Ah, no problem. You folks sound like you're from up north, so why not show y'all a bit of southern hospitality?"

Larry laughed. "Jeez, we really stick out that much?" he asked as they walked outside.

"Usually when folks show up in fancy cars with fancy clothes, they from up north." Gunner had a bit of venom in his words, but tried to cover it. "I work construction, so I love the northerners. House building has shot right up, yes siree." He pointed to a beat-up truck. "That's my truck. Just stick with me, and we'll get ya where y'all need to be."

Larry and Helen got in their car and buckled up.

"Larry, I don't like this," said Helen. She was nervous of the trio.

"Hel, relax. They're a bunch of kids on a beer run. We'll follow them to County Route 41, give them a beep and a wave, and be on our way. Besides, what are they going to do to us?" He smiled at his wife, trying to reassure her.

"I guess you're right. They just give me the creeps is all."

"Get used to it, sweetheart. These are our people now." He put the car in gear and followed the old truck.

The drive was going smoothly. Gunner kept his truck under the speed limit, allowing Larry to stick right behind him. Some of the roads were better than others, and they were on a road which had seen better days. It was desolate. There were no houses or streetlights.

Gunner pulled over and Nancy jumped out of the truck and began vomiting on the side of the road.

Larry looked at Helen and they both got out of the car.

"Is she okay?" asked Helen, walking towards the girl. After 40 years of teaching, Helen had developed a maternal instinct.

"She's fine," said Clint, the first words he said to them.

Larry didn't see Gunner, and he looked around for the skinny man. He didn't notice him sneaking up with a billy club in his hand.

Gunner hit Larry in the back of the head, dropping the older man to the cracked pavement.

"Hey, what the fuck?" Helen yelled, looking at her dazed husband lying on the roadway. She took a step towards him, but Clint and Nancy grabbed her. "Let me go, please," she whined, but they were already wrapping her hands in duct tape.

"Shut yer fucking yap," Nancy said, tearing off the last bit of tape with her teeth, which had seen better days.

Gunner stood over the injured man and grabbed his hands. "Toss me the tape." He held his hand out.

Nancy threw him the roll and Clint walked over to help.

"Helen?" Larry moaned, still dazed from the brutal strike to the head. There was no blood, but he seemed out of it.

"Quiet, old man," Gunner said as he wrapped Larry's wrists a few times and tore off the rest. "There, snug as a bug in a rug." He threw the tape to Clint.

Gunner dragged Larry over to his truck. He propped him up and waited for the man to regain his composure.

Helen screamed and kicked, but it was no use; the duct tape was tight.

Larry looked up at Gunner, who had his knife out.

"Welcome back," said Gunner, a smile on his face. He took a pack of smokes from his pocket and lit one. He blew the smoke into Larry's face. "I thought maybe I killed ya too soon."

"Wh-what do you want from us?" Larry, still dazed, asked. "Just take what you want, but please don't hurt us."

Gunner laughed and walked over to Helen. He dragged her over and sat her next to her husband.

"Whelp, I am gonna take what I want, you betcha. As for not hurting ya…" He grinned a wolfish grin and put the knife up to his face.

Clint was going through Larry's car, stuffing things in his pockets.

"Here's what's gonna happen. I'm gonna slit your throat." Gunner pointed to Larry with the knife. "Then, me and ole Clint are gonna fuck your wife. When we're done, we're gonna slit her throat. Then we're gonna take your bodies to the nearest swamp and feed ya to the gators. Your car will be chopped by the morning. How's that sound?"

Nancy was smiling. "Sounds good to me, Gunner. Do I get to have fun too?" she asked, trying to be sexy.

"Sure, baby. I'll give you yours when we get home," said Gunner.

Nancy looked dejected.

"But first we'll stop and get some ice, get fucked up, and I'll bang ya all night."

That sounded better.

"Clint, anything good?"

"Oh yeah, Gunner. We hit the motherload. Money, jewelry, credit cards. We eatin' good tonight," he yelled into the sky.

Larry was weeping. "Please, just let us go. We won't tell a soul, I promise. Take everything. Leave us here." He put his head down, sobbing. "We have children and grandchildren. Please, I beg you."

Gunner crouched down. "Damn, you are some kind of pussy," he laughed. "Crying like a baby. Listen, it's just business. Look at your wife, not a tear shed." He pointed the knife at Helen. "You're gonna be a fun lay, aren't cha?" he asked.

"Well, your way isn't working," Helen said to her husband. "Can we do my way now?" she asked.

"I guess," said Larry.

His face changed in an instant. The coy, weeping older man was gone. Looking out at Gunner was a beast, a denizen of myth and legend. He ripped through the layers of duct tape like it was wet tissue paper.

Gunner stared in shock, but quickly regained his composure. In fear, he stabbed out, his blade hitting Larry in the upper chest. It did nothing.

Larry's fingers were tipped in long, razor sharp claws. He slashed at Gunner's face.

The black claws flayed flesh and left etchings in Gunner's skull. His right eyeball fell victim to the attack, popping and weeping ocular fluid down his bloodied cheek.

"Ah!" Gunner screamed and reached up to cradle his ruined face. The knife went clattering on the broken road as he needed both hands to try and contain the misery.

Larry grabbed him by the throat. His unholy talons pierced the boy's soft neck, allowing life blood to run down his fingers. Lifting Gunner into the air as if he were a child and not a grown man, he said, "You were going to fuck my wife?" The jagged teeth filling his mouth made talking difficult. He spat with every word.

Gunner pulled at the demonic hand around his neck. The loss of blood and lack of oxygen were sending him into a frenzy. He was in panic mode and kicked at the beast in front of him. He didn't even notice he'd pissed his pants.

"I asked you a question. Were you going to fuck my wife?" Larry was nose to nose with the young man.

Gunner fought for air.

"I thought so," Larry said through gritted teeth. His free hand reached down to Gunner's crotch and found his shriveled cock and balls. The look of fear on the man's face, even with death imminent, was beautiful to Larry. He squeezed, feeling the delicate parts deform under his grasp.

His claws ripped through the piss-soaked denim and found flesh. “I think your fucking days are over.” Larry laughed as his talons dug into Gunner’s cock root. He tore and ripped the shriveled manhood from the crying man, casting it into the night air.

With a quick twist, Larry snapped Gunner’s neck and let his corpse fall wet and hard to the roadway.

Helen was crouched like a leopard waiting to pounce; and pounce she did. Her transformed legs launched her after Nancy, who thought she could get away. Helen landed on her back, driving the girl to the ground in a heap of screams.

Nancy’s left leg snapped at the shin, and a shock of white bone stuck out into the dark night.

Helen’s mouth, massive and bristling with teeth, clamped over Nancy’s face. The meth-head screamed into the hellish maw, feeling her own blood run down her throat.

Ripping at the girl’s face with no ceremony, Helen tore at her cheeks and pulled her jaw off in a snap of bone and tendon.

Nancy’s screams were wet and painful, but she was still alive…for the moment.

Helen spit the girl’s jaw onto the roadway and looked at her severed tongue wagging, trying to form words of anguish. She went back in, aiming for the soft throat. Her fangs made short work of Nancy’s bird-like neck as she bit and tore, showering the road in gore.

Larry and Helen, both covered in blood, stood near each other. They eyed Clint, who was frozen, and growled.

Clint watched as Larry and Helen approached from opposite sides. He pulled his knife from his belt and pointed the quivering tip at them in turn. "Stay the fuck back!" he muttered, trying to keep his eyes on the monsters in front of him, but he kept looking at the mangled corpses of his friends.

The couple circled, like the predators they were. Helen struck first. She came in low, swiping at his leg. Her claws cut through muscle like a hot knife through butter.

Clint swiped at her with his blade, but hit nothing but air. His leg gave out, but he still stood. He felt no pain, though his leg was weak. He looked down and saw his shredded muscle, red in the headlights of the vehicles.

Larry took the opportunity and attacked. He plunged his claws into Clint's upper arm.

The electric shock of pain made Clint drop the knife, and his attention snapped to the beast attached to him. The blade seemed to fall in slow motion, clattering to the ground.

Tightening his grip, Larry dug into the bone and ripped. The arm came off in a heap of jagged meat and broken bone. Arterial blood sprayed, but he didn't seem to mind.

Helen grabbed Clint's head, her claws digging into his bald pate. She twisted violently enough to make his spine pop from the base of his skull.

The fat man collapsed in a heap.

Larry and Helen relaxed, allowing their bodies to resume human form.

Looking around, surveying the damage he and his wife had done, Larry joked, “So much for southern hospitality.”

Helen smiled and flicked blood from her hands. “Yeah, I’d say so.”

Larry’s phone dinged. He wiped his hand as best as he could on his pants and pulled his cell phone from his pocket. “Fuck,” he muttered.

“Problem?” Helen asked, stepping up to his shoulder.

“The movers dumped everything in the living room and left.” He locked his phone and put it away.

The blood was tacky and starting to dry on his clothes and flesh. “Well, we’d better clean up and get going.” He started back towards their car. “We have a ton of moving to do.”

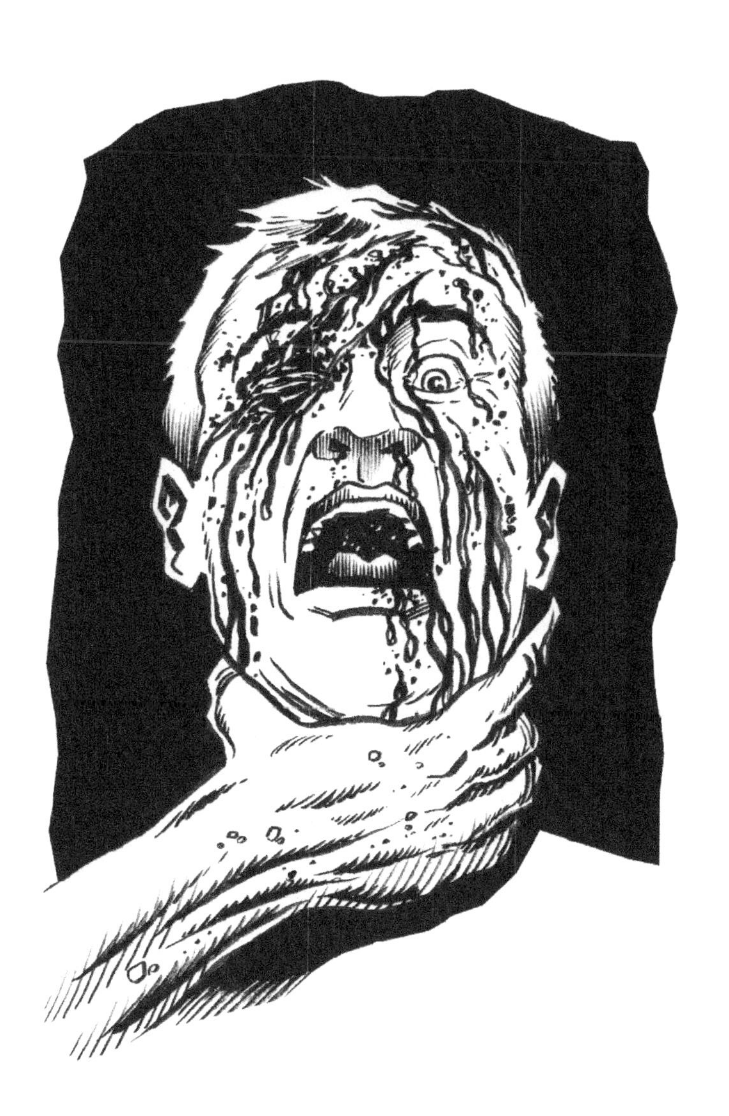

DIE HIVE SCUM

Skeever ran, ducking as he did. He narrowly dodged a wire that had been drawn across the alley. Frantic, he hurdled a pile of filth—the remnants of a ruptured sewer main somewhere deep in the hive city of NeeTeer.

He slipped on a rather nasty lump of shit, nearly causing him to lose his balance in the muck, but he held firm and continued his sprint. People—well, mostly human inhabitants—skittered out of his way. Those who were slow, or just immobile, were pushed by the fleeing man.

"The fuck out of my way," Skeever grunted, throwing a young boy with reptilian-looking skin to the floor.

The boy hit the dank ground, splashing in filth. His eyes, which blinked vertically, closed in shock as the rogue leaped over him.

Skeever didn't look back, but he could hear the slapping of the Detective's boots as they continued their chase. He wasn't built for too much physical activity. Maybe a quick sprint here and there to escape the market guards from time to time, but not a full-on pursuit. And Skeever knew the Detectives were a breed unlike any other, much more determined than a basic guard. Where a guard might crack your skull with a length of pipe, a Detective would put a hardshot into your brain. If they were brave enough, they might even carry a ray gun. But the super-heated burst of light was dangerous, especially so deep in the hive where noxious fumes could ignite if your shot was errant.

Where Skeever ran—below the 82nd level—was a danger on its own. Re-breather masks were a must for someone not used to the corrupt air, and the deeper you went, the worse the air quality. Not that anywhere in NeeTeer was safe, but the further down, the worse off you were.

Skeever rubbed at the goggles covering his eyes. Each breath was a fight through the mask and tasted of harsh chemicals. He needed a new filter months ago, but couldn't quite get his hands on one. With what he had tucked in his vest, he didn't think he'd ever have to worry about credits again. That was if he lived to sell it. Normally, Skeever stayed above the 82nd level, but as a man with many gifts and no fucks to give, he would take almost any job, even those that brought him deeper into the hive city.

The dirty glass smudged as he wiped at it, but enough was clear for him to see an avenue of escape, at least he hoped. Growing up on the 97th level, Skeever would often venture lower into the hive, but rarely dip below the 82nd.

When his parents died in the hive war of BT420, Skeever was left alone. None of his siblings had lived past childhood thanks to their horrific mutations. He knew if he was going to survive hive life, he had to make it on his own. Skeever was always sharp as a boy, but the lack of nutrition and exposure to toxic sludge had stunted his development. Not that he was the only child with birth defects, but some of them were the lucky ones. At least in hive life. Some kids, like the reptilian boy he'd shoved moments earlier, mutated. Many of them were doomed to die painful deaths, but some adapted and thrived. Whether it was the ability to breathe noxious fumes without so much as a cough, to see in the darkness only found in a hive world, or the growth of extra limbs, these mutants were often revered or feared. Sometimes it was both. Skeever was blessed with a lack of muscle mass and a pair of lungs that pained him during rough activity. But, at least he was alive, which was more than he could say for his brothers and sisters.

A mutated old man, whose testicles were the size of small children, sat in a crude wheelchair. Each wheel was a different size and dimension, making the man lean to one side. He was against the wall of the narrow street, sitting next to an open grill pit. Flames licked at the metal grate, hissing as they charred some kind of mystery meat.

Another man, presumably his son, stood behind the grill, manning the food and monitoring the hive scum lurking around.

Skeever's stomach growled, but he couldn't think of food at that moment. He could use the fire, though. That, and the old man.

The old man looked as Skeever charged. His rheumy eyes widened just as the rogue plowed into him, sending him, and his enormous sack, into the grill. He must've had some kind of combustible salve on his scrotum, because he burst into flames, starting down below. Scraps of meat went flying as he thrashed.

Mongrels came out of the shadows, rushing to eat the meat, some of which was their brethren. The bony dogs snapped and snarled, biting each other almost as much as the cooked meat.

Derelicts and scamps pushed each other, fighting the dogs for scraps of food as the young man tried his best to fight them off. It was no use, and he backed away just before a girl, whose face was horribly burned, stabbed at his gut with a sliver of metal.

Not one of them stopped to help the old man, who was still screaming as he burned—such is hive life. His charred corpse would be pulled, and the Reclaimers would be called. And he, like everyone else who died in the hive, would be fed into the reactor, keeping the hive alive for just a moment longer.

Skeever didn't stay to watch his handiwork, but the screams and yells were more than enough. The rogue changed direction, planting his boots as he did so. One of the blessed features of NeeTeer was the exhaust ducts everywhere. Gas and fumes had to flow somehow, and most of the noxious material would run through the vent systems. Many vents had been destroyed over the years, leaving them open spaces for the horrors of the hive to live, but to Skeever they offered an opportunity. An open vent called to him. It was pitch black beyond what he could see, but it was either take his chances with what lurked beneath, or a hardshot to the head from the pursuing Detectives.

He gave a glance behind, just for a fraction of a second, to see if the Detectives were on his trail. The only indication was that people were still screaming, begging for help as the fire spread.

A crack rang out, echoing through the narrow street. One Detective must've lost his patience with the sub-humans and let them know it at the end of his gun. This only elicited more screams, but Skeever knew his time was running out.

He took one deep, chemically-tainted breath through his mask, and slithered into the vent. Instinctively, he touched his vest, making sure his treasure was still there. If it wasn't, the run was all for naught, and he was dead anyway. Few people could steal from Sardom Senk and live to tell about it. Even though what Skeever stole from Senk was already stolen, it didn't matter. Once something was in the mechanically augmented hands of Sardom Senk, it was his.

The entrance to the pipe was wet. Skeever slithered on his belly, but he could sense that the pipe was taller than he thought. Slowly, he stood, hunching over as his head hit the ceiling. For once in his life, he was lucky to have his growth stunted so much. He shuffled forward in the dark, hoping to find a bend in the tunnel so he could activate the light built into his mask, and hoped to find nothing waiting for him in the darkness.

***

Detective Krut Gast and Detective Benj Akara stopped running. Each had a gun in hand and was looking for anything to shoot, especially some hive scum. The masks covering their faces weren't quite top-of-the-line, but their filters were new and fresh. Each man gazed at the grainy digital display that flashed over the right lens of their goggles. Teal writing danced, relaying the same message to each man: their target was no longer in range. The toggle on their left lens blipped as if searching, but showed no sign of locking onto anything.

The crowd was dispersing after Gast fired a warning shot into the air, but still, their goggles hadn't been able to find their target.

Detective Gast reached up and switched off the monitoring device on his goggles, prompting Akara to do the same.

"Fuck," Gast muttered. His voice was filtered through the speaker attached to the front of the apparatus. His breath was ragged, and his fingers looked for the oxygen infuser.

With a hiss, his mask mixed a shot of pure oxygen into the system, instantly helping him catch his breath. His partner wasn't as lucky. Akara's mask was a bit more worn. The O2 function on his had long since been broken, but he was younger, so he'd be fine; and if he wasn't, Gast didn't much care.

Akara stood up straight and took a deep breath. He'd only been a Detective for two years; this was only his sixth time venturing below the 82nd level. Even though he had young lungs, he didn't much like trying to breathe through the masks. He'd never tell Gast that.

"Where the fuck did he go?" asked Akara. He held his gun, but had it pointed at the ground.

The commotion of the chase had died down, and the hivers began slowly returning to their miserable lives. The streets were filling with bodies again, since the gunfire and chase had ceased.

A rich odor of burned flesh wafted through the air, and both Detectives knew the corpse of the old man was the source. Still, it didn't help that he smelled pretty good. Especially since they'd not eaten much in the way of fresh food in a while.

Most people thought being a Detective was a life of luxury. Well, they were wrong.

Gast had been a member of the organization for the better part of a decade, and had to crawl out from underneath the thumb of many creditors. It didn't help that his love for whores and gambling on mutant fights were the main hemorrhages of his credits.

Even with the meager salary, being a Detective came with perks, one of which was authority. The organization wasn't quite sanctioned like the district guard units were, but they were well known throughout the hive city. While the guards were dedicated to peace, order, and extortion in their local neighborhoods, the Detectives were men for hire. Need someone found? Call the Detectives. Need that same person killed and tossed into the acid pits? Also, call the Detectives. There wasn't much they wouldn't do for a stack of credits, and murder was one of their best products. Of course, they did other stuff, like kidnapping, extortion, arson, or just plain old assault. The top dogs in their group liked money, and hired men and women who had no qualms about getting dirty—either with actual dirt and blood, or any other filth in NeeTeer.

Gast preferred blood, especially someone else's, but he'd spilled quite a bit of his own over the years. Feeling refreshed after his O2 boost, he holstered his weapon, prompting Akara to do the same.

The streets wriggled with hivers, many getting too close to the Detectives.

"Stay back," Gast said to an old woman.

She didn't wear a mask, as her lungs were used to the air that deep in the hive. Her face was wrinkled, and a tan fluid ran down the creases in her old skin. Gast didn't see a wound; it was as if her flesh was secreting the noxious goop.

"A credit to spare?" she mumbled with a mouth devoid of teeth. Even her gums looked rotten.

Gast wasn't stupid enough to transfer a credit to the old crone. He had a few credit chips in his pocket, but giving them to one piece of hive scum would only open the floodgates for the rest of them. He'd rather give her a hardshot to the face. From behind his goggles, he could see more of them looking at him and Akara. The Detectives were a feared bunch, but outnumbered fifty to one, Gast knew the situation could turn on them in an instant.

Firm, but not too harsh, he thought.

The crowd was getting tighter around him, and he could feel little hands plucking at his clothing, searching. He wasn't that dumb. All of his loose credits were sewn into pouches deep in his pockets. But the last thing he wanted to lose was his ID. It was the only reason he could traverse the levels so easily. He didn't want to get stuck below the 82nd level, what most people referred to as the 'underhive'.

"No credits," he said through the voice modulator.

The sound of his voice made other ears perk up. The only ones who wore masks were upperhivers. It was as if the population had forgotten about the chase only moments before, and the fact these two men carried guns. They realized it wasn't a gang of Detectives, but only two. Gast knew things could go bad in a hurry and he and Akara needed to get the fuck out of there.

Akara had his own issues to contend with. A group of mutated children surrounded him. They were laughing with dangling tongues and cleft palates, but older ones didn't. No, those mutated little shits had watery eyes filled with malice.

A girl, no older than fourteen, was missing a good chunk of her hair. A wrinkled, pink scar replaced the mud-colored hair, and a dirty hand hid in her shirt. Gast didn't have to be an alchemist to know she was holding a weapon. If the girl drew a weapon, even a crude knife, he'd have to kill her.

There was no mercy for those who fought the Detectives. And if a Detective showed mercy or weakness, they would die at the hands of their superiors. If they were going to walk away and continue their pursuit of the hive scum, Gast needed to do something.

He took a deep breath, sucking the remnants of the O2 through the filter before reaching for the clasps. With a hiss, he broke the seals on his re-breather. "Everyone, back the fuck up!" he yelled, devoid of the mask.

The underhivers looked at him and froze. Most upperhivers wouldn't dare expose themselves to the fumes and air below the 82nd level, but Gast had little choice.

An old woman paused, looking up at him.

Gast had his hand on his gun, but didn't draw it. Instead, he reached into a hidden pouch and pulled out his ID. It wasn't a fancy holo-ID like some bosses had, but it was still impressive to the hive scum. Gast pressed his thumb to the small print reader on the ID.

The chip beeped as it came to life and a robotic voice spoke. *"Gast, Krut. Detective, grade 3. Time of service, 9 years and 7 months, standard time. Jobs completed 215 out of 216 possible. 1 open case. Confirmed kills, 789.*"

The crowd looked at him. Gast was never called handsome, but he occasionally didn't have to pay for sex. Those girls weren't the best looking, but if he could save a few credits, that was a plus. His face was full, but far from fat. Deep-set, gray eyes were buried under bushy eyebrows. Gast had a permanent scowl, which caused the leathery skin of his forehead to crease. His hair was once blonde, but in his later years, it had faded and grayed.

"We," Gast pointed to Akara, who was still trying to fend off the greedy children, "are on Detective business. Official business," he said. "Now, the problems of the agency aren't your problems, but you know that can change. If you don't let us pass and hinder us, they will become your problems." Gast slipped his mask back over his face. He was never so happy to breathe the chemical-flavored air.

The crowd sneered and grumbled. Faceless agitators yelled with anonymity, but that was about it. With ease, the crowd could kill both men and strip them of their worldly belongings. They'd even get away with their IDs and using the Detectives' severed thumbs for a while. But more Detectives would come, and then the entire street, maybe even the neighborhood, would be massacred, and not nicely either. Below the 82nd level, the law was more lax, especially to the residents. Even the guardsmen wouldn't try to stop a regiment of Detectives, especially if they were equipped with battle armor, which they certainly would be.

"Excuse me, Mr. Detective?" a voice said from the crowd.

The rest of the hivers looked toward the speaker.

Gast and Akara did the same.

A girl—a small, sickly-looking thing—waded through the mass of bodies. Her clothes were patchwork, and she had a rash under her nose. The pink bumps were wet, but Gast didn't know if it was snot, or if they were oozing; he didn't care.

"Yes," Gast said, again speaking through the robotic voice of his modulator.

"Your man, the skinny man you were chasin', he went thataway," she said. The girl pointed a dirty finger down a side street.

Gast looked to where the girl was pointing, not knowing if he should trust the hive urchin. It could've been a ploy just to get them away and out of their hair, or the girl could've been telling the truth. His gut hadn't served him wrong in almost the decade he'd been a Detective. Gast scanned the crowd, looking for the glare of guilt and acknowledgment. Others saw their target as well, but none were as brave as the little girl in front of him. Gast smiled, but it was for naught. The girl couldn't see his mouth behind the mask, only his eyes, and the smile didn't reach them.

"You know, it's a crime to lie to a Detective." It wasn't, but she didn't know that. He crouched down to eye level with the girl.

"Oh, I know it," she said. "But I'm not lying."

Up close, Gast realized the rash was weeping fluid, not covered in snot. Tiny corpuscles dripped from white heads on her face. He moved closer to her, thankful for his mask. Gast had his inoculations, but one could never be too careful in the lower levels of the hive.

He reached into his pocket, pulled out a credit chip, and held it in front of the girl's face.

Her mud-colored eyes lit up, and dozens of others stared with greed.

He may have just signed her death warrant if she didn't have a family member with her, a family member who was ready to kill if needed.

She took the chip with her dirty fingers and pocketed it quickly. Without another word, she fled into the crowd, clutching the credit to her small chest.

Gast looked around at the faces, most of which were mutated. His gaze landed on the old woman. “Now, me and my partner aren’t going to have any problems, are we?” Gast, feeling a bit more confident in his position, placed a hand on his gun.

She wrinkled her nose as if he stunk. If his body odor could overpower the stench of them, he’d be shocked. Without a word, she shook her head and stepped aside.

Gast looked at Akara, who finally was able to shoo the kids away. Hopefully, they had stolen nothing important. “Come on,” he said and started toward where girl pointed.

Akara drew his gun and followed.

The chase was back on.

***

The power cell in Skeever’s light was at half charge. He’d have to add a new one to the long list of things to buy. If only he could escape the fucking Detectives, he might have a chance to sell what he’d stolen.

Another big if.

There was a good chance Sardom Senk already put a bounty on the item, meaning anyone who recovered it would get a handsome reward. And anyone caught with it could face death, or even worse, be sold to the slavers of the deep hive.

The deep hive made the underhive look like a street fair. The worst of the worst lived in the deep hive, buried under thousands of tons of buildings and bodies. Power was sparse, at best, and most of the mutants living in the deep hive had augmented vision to allow them to see in the dark. It was one place in NeeTeer where few dared to tread, even the Detectives. But, if one was brave enough to make the journey, anything could be found. Illicit goods, narcotics, flesh, weapons, assassins—anything and everything lurked in the deep hive. Most outsiders who ventured down didn't make it back. If they did, it usually wasn't whole.

Skeever shivered at the thought of going to the deep hive. The underhive was far enough for him and even then, he didn't know if he was going to make it out in one piece. At that moment, Skeever would've killed for a deep hiver's night vision. The bulb in his light was fading quickly.

It had been nearly an hour since he lost the Detectives in the street. Every few minutes, he paused and listened, praying he didn't hear them giving chase, or even worse, something else lurking in the pipes.

Most of the pipes in the hive city were connected. Whether it was a waste line, gas line, or just a vent, somewhere they all intersected. Skeever left the original vent he'd escaped into, and was in the wide sewer tunnel. It smelled worse, but was much bigger, so big he could walk, albeit with a slight hunch. That was fine by him. At least he could make good time and put some distance behind him.

Skeever stopped not only to listen, but to catch his breath. The adrenaline was wearing off, and he realized how tired he was. It seemed like ages since he stole the item from Sardom Senk. An item he had no intention of using, but didn't quite know who to sell it to. Hell, he didn't even know if it was real, but he was going to find out, and quickly.

Finding the driest patch of sewer pipe he could find, he sat and dug through his inner pocket. The item was still there, but he had to look at it one more time. Skeever pulled it out, impressed again with the heft of such a small item. He held it in front of the…

"…way. I can smell the hive scum," a voice echoed down the tunnel.

No! Skeever's mind erupted. *How the fuck did they find me?*

He crammed the item back into his jacket. Next to it, hanging in a shoulder holster, was his last hope. The ray gun was an old model, a model which hadn't been produced in centuries, but it was the only form of protection he had. He didn't even know if it still had a charge, or if it would fire without killing him, but it was better than what the Detectives would do to him.

The tunnel veered to the left about a hundred paces away. If he could run it without using his light, he might have a chance. Painfully, he clicked off his headlamp and ran as quickly as he dared. Skeever's fingers rubbed the slimy wall, searching for that tunnel entrance. He did his best to not think about what he might be touching. With some of the credits he was going to earn, he'd be buying a nice long shower, with actual water.

His fingers slid, finding the smooth entrance to the tunnel. Skeever splashed in the filth, which was deeper than the main tunnel he was in. The muck was the consistency of porridge, and cold. Again, he forced from his mind what it might be, but even his filter couldn't take away the entire stench.

Skeever's breath was ragged, and he was getting dizzy. The running was killing him, but he knew the alternative. He wished he had a mutation. One that was helpful, not just one that made him sickly.

He stopped, allowing his heart to slow down. He wanted to rip the mask off in the worst way, but knew that was a bad idea. Not only didn't he know what shit he was calf-deep in, but he did not know what fumes were floating around, and the mask helped quiet his rough breathing. If he didn't have it on, his gasping breaths would be heard two levels up. Slowly, he did his best to regain his composure. In the darkness, he sat, listening for the sounds of pursuit. The sound which he never heard.

***

Gast wanted to use white light in the tunnel, but he knew better. The element of surprise was always the best, especially when cornering your target. The last thing he wanted was for the hive scum to know they were coming and run or fight.

Actually, he didn't mind a fight. It made things interesting, that was for sure.

Akara hadn't had many fights, so a good scrap in a tunnel would bring up his credibility with the rest of the Detectives if he survived it.

Gast didn't like the night vision that was equipped with their masks, but he knew it was the best option. He wasn't sure if they were on the right path, but he knew how to flush targets out. When he yelled about being able to smell the hive scum, he stopped and listened. Sure as shit, he heard the telltale splashing and frantic running of his target.

They were in hot pursuit once again. The rush of adrenaline surged through his body, knowing they were getting closer.

Scanning the area with his night vision, an array of tunnels lay before them, some smaller than others, but each of them big enough to hide the hive scum.

Akara stood by Gast and looked as well, but neither man saw anything.

Their target was a little smarter than they gave him credit for. Even after flushing him out, the man hadn't turned on a white light. It was doubtful his re-breather mask was equipped with night vision as well, but Gast wasn't sure, so they listened as the man quietly splashed away from them.

Gast closed his eyes, cutting out the orange glow of his night vision, and listened. He pressed one hand against the tunnel wall, not caring about the putrid slime that greased his palm.

"I—"

"Shh," Gast said, cutting his partner off. He snapped his eyes open, letting the orange glow of his night vision flood his sight. "Come on. This way."

Without another word, the Detectives silently stalked through the tunnels. They were closing in for the kill.

***

Skeever heard nothing. Finally, he was alone, or so he thought. Slowly, he reached up and snapped on the white light of his mask.

The Detectives stood in front of him, both with guns drawn. Their goggles gave off an orange hue, but that quickly disappeared. White light shot from their masks, holding Skeever in place.

"This shit has gone on long enough, hive scum," Gast said. "Now, we've been sent to recover what you've stolen, so give it here."

Skeever stared into the barrels of their guns. They were hardshot guns, firing metal bullets as opposed to the ray gun he had holstered under his vest. There was no way out alive. These men would steal the item and leave him dead; just another dead hiver in a tunnel, food for the rats and mutants roaming the dark. His hand itched. He wanted to draw his ray gun and fire, hoping to take at least one of the Detectives with him in death, but he wasn't a gunfighter. He was a rogue, an urchin who roamed the streets. Or, as the Detectives called him, hive scum. Still, he had to think of something, some way to escape with his skin.

Thinking back to all the scraps he'd been in since childhood, he knew this was, by far, the worst. His hand went towards his vest, inching closer to not only the precious item, but his ray gun.

"Ah, ah, not so fast," Gast said. "My partner, Detective Akara, will help you find the missing item." He nodded towards Skeever, sending the younger man into motion.

Skeever didn't listen to Gast. His fingers touched the pitted handle of the ray gun. His heart thumped like the sound of a rickety train.

"Listen," he said. His fingers bypassed the gun and found their way into the hidden pouch, wrapping around the item. "This *thing* is important. Too important for the likes of us, no offense. Not to mention, it's valuable, so much so that all three of us would never have to work another day in our lives. The amount of credits we could get for this, plus the leverage; hell, we might even get influence over members living in the Steel Cloud cities.

Skeever didn't truly believe that Steel Clouders would ever associate with them, but it was worth a shot. The massive, man-made cities hovered above the planet. A dual atmosphere lent itself to the buoyancy of the sprawling cities, helping to keep them aloft and away from the nuclear pollution of the surface world—another layer of separation in their cruel world.

Gast laughed and aimed. "Oh yes, let me trust my life to the likes of a fucking thief. If anything besides the item comes out of your pocket, you're fucking dead."

Skeever held the item but didn't pull it free. "What does it matter?" he yelled. His voice echoed down the tunnel. It was muffled by his mask, but still, the sound traveled. "You're just going to kill me anyway."

Even though Skeever couldn't see Gast's mouth, he knew the man was smiling just by his eyes.

"Well, yes, but I would at least give you the decency of a hardshot in the back of the head. It's the least I can do for your cooperation."

Akara had his gun trained on Skeever's heart as he stepped closer. "Give it here," he said, his hand outstretched.

Skeever wrapped his hand around the item and pulled it out. "This is it. Is this what you want?" he asked. Snot welled up in his mask as he cried in frustration. He knew it would come to this one day, but he hoped it would be a little later in life.

Akara took another step forward. "Give it to me and get on your fucking knees." His voice wavered through the voice modulator on his mask.

Skeever thought he might still have a chance, albeit a minor one. "Take it," he said, as the item fumbled from his hands and into the muck of the sewer.

"Fucker," Akara said, as he bent down to grab it.

It was only for a second, but Gast's eyes broke, and look towards his partner.

Reaching back into his vest, Skeever pulled the ray gun free. He knew discharging the antique weapon in such a tight space would probably kill them all, but didn't care. At least he wouldn't die alone. The weapon hummed in his hand as he turned it on, making the bones vibrate with power.

Akara, with the sludge-covered item in his hand, looked up as the coils surrounding the barrel of the ray gun glowed blue with electricity. He jumped to his feet as the air crackled with the release of power.

A flash of light erupted from the barrel of the old weapon and into the Detective's belly. White hot pain erupted in Akara's gut as he splashed down into the filth of the sewer.

Skeever had never killed a man, but he knew there would be more killing soon if he didn't take care of Detective Gast.

"Die, hive scum!" Gast yelled as his big gun barked in the confines of the tunnel.

Angry hardshots flew past Skeever, but none struck him.

The ray gun was hot and shaking. He wasn't much of a weapons expert, but something told him the gun was overcharging. He was holding a ticking time bomb. Skeever snapped the barrel towards Gast, who was still firing at him. Something stung

Skeever's stomach and chest, but it couldn't have been hardshots, at least, that's what he thought. There was no pain, just a slight bit of pressure.

The coils were glowing an obnoxious blue, begging for a release of the power they were holding back.

Skeever pressed the trigger, sending forth a ray of super-hot light.

The shot went wide, missing the Detective. It tore through the roof of the tunnel, burning through one of the many hidden pipes carrying various gases throughout the hive city. A gout of fire sprayed from the roof, right into Gast's face.

Gast screamed as his mask burned, melting to his skin. He dropped his gun and ripped the mask away. Flesh and rubber were married together in a hellish taffy, as he was burned nearly to the bone. His left ear peeled off, as did most of his cheek, leaving his teeth exposed. With no other option, Gast fell to the ground and buried his ruined face in the cold, putrid sludge running through the tunnel.

Skeever looked at the ray gun in awe, nearly forgetting it was about to explode. Not a second too soon, he threw the gun, hoping to land it in the lap of the burned Detective. Never the strong one, Skeever's throw was off, and the vibrating ray gun fell short, plopping in the muck. With a hiss and crack, the smell of ozone ripped through the tunnel.

The ray gun exploded, but the sludge contained most of the blast. A flash of white light and a spray of excrement decorated the walls of the sewer.

Flames from the ruptured gas line still burned bright, giving Skeever enough light to see his escape route. He cranked up the intensity of the white light on his mask and ran, leaving the item behind. Part of him wanted to grab it and still see if he could still make something off of it, but he didn't even know if it survived the electric blast. For all he knew, it was destroyed or rendered useless. He may still be a wanted man, but hopefully the bounty would be removed from his head. That was doubtful, as he knew the vengeance of Sardom Senk was far and wide, but the odds of surviving were much better without the fucking item.

It didn't matter, Skeever had beaten the odds once again. And, once again, he was on the run, but no one was chasing him, not yet, anyway.

He stopped and dimmed the light. He remembered the gunfight with the Detective and hadn't thought to check himself for damage. Over the years, he'd heard of people being shot or stabbed and not feeling a thing. Adrenaline can do weird things to a body, and if he was shot, he needed to do something immediately.

Skeever touched his body but felt no wounds. He looked at his hands in the light, inspecting them for any traces of blood. Nothing. Again, he rubbed his hands over his belly and stopped. His shirt had holes in it, a whole mess of them. Something else was stuck behind the fabric, hard lumps of something.

Lifting his shirt, half a dozen deformed hardshots fell into the muck. He grabbed one before it fell and held it up to the light. It was mushed and twisted as if it had been shot into armor. He tossed it, along with the other ones, and inspected his chest. Nothing, not a single bruise. His skin had stopped the hardshots.

Skeever smiled and tucked his shirt back in. He ran down the tunnel toward freedom, grinning the entire way. He had a helpful mutation after all.

***

Gast was in agony. His face was a charred and melted mess, but he was alive. He'd survive the wound, that he knew, but he didn't know how long he'd be able to survive in the fetid darkness inhaling the dank fumes of the underhive.

Akara gasped and shuddered. The light on the front of his mask was the only light left in the tunnel since the gas fire burned out.

Gast walked over to his injured partner. The ray gun had done a number on the young Detective. A charred hole the size of a child's fist sat oozing gore in Akara's belly. He wheezed and gasped, each breath bringing pain to his goggled eyes.

Ripping a piece of burned sleeve from his shirt, Gast covered his mouth. The fumes were burning his eyes, and he was getting dizzy. He knew he had only one option if he wanted to survive.

"Sorry, friend," he said as he crouched down next to Akara and pulled the Detective's gun from his hand. The realization of impending death can make a man act out of sorts. Gast had seen it many times before.

Akara tried to resist, but his energy was all but sapped.

Gast checked the gun, ensuring it was loaded. He holstered it and plucked the spare magazines from Akara's belt as well.

Akara's eyes were wide. His ragged breath was loud through the modulator as Gast began pulling at the latches of the mask. Weakly, Akara swatted at Gast's hands, but there was no strength left in the parry.

Gast pulled the mask from his partner's face and quickly put it over his own. He secured it, wishing it could dump a shot of O2 as his did. It didn't matter. The chemical taste of the filter was like heaven compared to the stench of the sewer. The mask hurt his burned face, but he'd have to suffer the pain. It was what drove him. Pain. Whether it was inflicted upon him, or him inflicting it upon others, it drove him.

He didn't speak; there was no need to. There was only one option remaining for his partner. He drew the gun and aimed at Akara's tear-streaked face. Gast never truly realized how young the man was, but the fear of death made every man look like a babe.

The gunshot was loud. Akara's forehead split as the hardshot ripped through his skull. Overpressure forced blood from his nose and eyes, making him weep gore. His brain matter mixed with the slurry of human waste and industrial grime.

Gast stared at the dead man who was once his partner. For a moment, he forgot why they were there, why he was looking at the canoed head of a fellow Detective. And then, he looked at Akara's other hand.

The item—the reason Gast was in the hellhole of the underhive. He didn't even know what the fuck the item was, or why it was so valuable, but it was his job to recover it. Sardom Senk had paid good money for their services. Gast held it in front of the light. It was wrapped in fabric, but it had some heft to it. Slowly, he unwrapped it and froze.

He could only stare. It took his chest tightening to realize he hadn't been breathing. There were very few things in the world that stole the breath from Krut Gast. Gently, he wrapped the item back up and secured it in a pouch he kept on his belt. It felt like he had a nuclear bomb on his waist. The power of the item weighed him down mentally rather than physically. He didn't know the value of it in terms of credits, but he knew it could change the course of existence for NeeTeer and all the other hive cities on the planet.

Gast wasn't a righteous man by any stretch of the imagination, but the item was far too valuable to return to Sardom Senk, nor would he return it to its original owner. He didn't know what he was going to do with it, but he knew having it would put a bounty on his head. It would bring forth more pain and death to those that hunted him. Of that, he was certain.

Krut Gast walked through the tunnels by the light of his mask. He needed to get back to civilization above the dreaded 82nd level of his home city of NeeTeer. But, more importantly, he needed a surgeon to fix his face. And then, maybe a drink and a whore. The scum and mercenaries of the entire hive city would be after him once they found out he had the item. Soon, they'd all know his name, and his mangled face would be the last thing they saw as he ushered them into death.

STRAWBERRY SHORTCAKE

I burst into the porta-potty about to shit my pants. I fumble with my button as I take a glance into the quagmire of filth and excrement. Mounds of feces and islands of blue toilet paper litter the cesspool. Something catches my eye, something I haven't tasted in a while…something delicious.

The maxi pad was resting on log the size of my wrist. It was a soaker, bursting with rich period blood and meaty clots. My mouth begins to water, flashbacks of stolen maxi pads from my mother's garbage had me drooling.

I fall to my knees and my jeans soak up a puddle of piss. The stench coming from the hole was repulsive, but I block it out, thinking only of warm, salty cunt-blood. I could almost feel the slimy clots in my mouth. I put my arms on the sides of the rim and push my face towards the slurry. My mouth is inches from my reward, so close my nose brushes a clump of gore. It was a delicious looking morsel resembling an errant drop of grape jelly. I stick my tongue out, seeking the middle of the pad. I know the best and thickest filling of a strawberry shortcake is in the center. The taste was divine, but a bitter tang gives me a little bit of a shock; this woman had a rather nasty yeast infection. I pull back and look, noticing a healthy shmear of lumpy cream mixed in with the bloody mucus. The tang and salt brought a smile to my face and I couldn't wait. I licked it again, this time digging the tip of my tongue into the mush. I scraped, letting my tongue fill with discharge and kept it curled so I didn't waste a glob. It was delicious, sour…and wriggly. Apparently, this lady had a case of the creepy crawlies along with her infection. Tiny worms squirmed through the cottage cheese-like discharge, tickling my taste buds. I pull my tongue, now full of cunt-cream, blood and vermin, back into my mouth. I ran the goop over my teeth and gums, the worms trying to dig into my flesh. I swallow the mixture, embracing the burn of the yeast infection in my throat.

With that mouthful gone, I can't wait any longer, I need to eat. I lean back in and wrap my mouth around the strawberry shortcake. With my teeth dug into the bloody cotton, I yank it free from the lump of shit holding it in place. I begin to chew.

Filth pours from my mouth. THIS IS HEAVEN. The foul, rancid liquid rushes down my chin and every time I bite, more and more enters my throat. I reach up and fold the edges of the pad, cramming the whole thing into my mouth. The viscous fluid gushes from my lips and nose. I gag when one of the wings of the pad tickles my throat. A torrent of vomit erupts, but I hold fast, not letting my strawberry shortcake go. A combination of funnel cake, cunt-blood, discharge and worms, flood my mouth. I chew, mixing blood clots with my sweet and sour vomit and squeeze every drop from the pad, before I swallow again. This time I hope everything stays down. The left-overs were thick and meaty, like roadkill blended with a bucket of loogies.

"Hey, are you almost done in there?" Some impatient asshole yells.

Huh, in my bliss I had forgotten to shit. Oh well, the porta-potty has a little more room, thanks to my love of strawberry shortcakes.

THE CUT OF YOUR JIB

"I don't like the cut of your jib."

Those eight words made Mark's blood run cold. He'd heard his father say them before, and each time, things got worse and worse. A shiver ran through his body, a shiver of knowing something bad was going to happen.

"No siree, that smart fucking mouth of yours got you in trouble yet again, Mark," Conrad said, looking at his son.

Ruthanne sat next to her big brother in the kitchen of their small house. She had seen the bad side of their father before, but she was only eight and hadn't *really* seen—until then. Ruthanne looked back and forth between her brother and father. There was no yelling, only words, but those words carried weight. It was almost a physical thing she could reach out and touch. Something bad was going to happen to Mark and she started to cry.

Mark, even though he was on the receiving end of his father's ire, reached out and patted his sister on the thigh. It wasn't much, but more than enough to stifle her tears…for a time.

Conrad looked at his boy, his only son, and sucked his teeth in a hiss. Each moment the boy looked at him was an affront to his manhood. His son had disrespected him, even if he didn't mean to. It didn't matter in Conrad's world; disrespect to one's parent was a serious crime with a heavy punishment.

If Annie was still alive, the disrespect would've been even worse. She was always one to coddle the kids, not discipline them.

Well, Conrad was in charge, and by God, his kids would listen, or else.

Mark was about to find out what *or else* meant. He shifted in the rigid kitchen chair. His ass was sweating and starting to itch. Sometimes, when he was nervous, he broke out in hives. He hoped that wasn't the case. The punishment was going to be bad enough without him needing to get medication for a rash.

Rubbing his stubble-strewn face, Conrad sighed. He was only forty-three, but looked like he was in his sixties. Years of farm work and hitting the bottle would do that, not to mention the pack of cigarettes he sucked down daily. He always wondered where their money was going, as he bought another carton of cancer sticks.

"What am I going to do with you, boy?" he said to his teenage son. "You're almost a man and you need a man's punishment." His eyes looked like they were welling with tears, but Conrad always looked like that, like he was always on the verge of crying over his dead wife, or a bad harvest, or even his kids, who he felt hated him.

"I know," he said, with an almost eureka-like moment, then walked out of the kitchen and into the small bathroom just past the living room.

Ruthanne knew she shouldn't talk, not when Conrad was mad, but she couldn't help it. Shaking, she turned to her brother. “What’s Daddy gonna do to you?” she asked, her little voice almost a whisper.

Mark truly didn’t know. He only knew it was going to be bad. The last time his father didn’t like the cut of his jib, he proceeded to put out a pack of cigarettes on Mark’s bare skin. When he was asked about the pain and burns, Mark lied and told everyone he was stung by a bunch of wasps.

The kids in his neighborhood knew better; some of their fathers were just as bad, or worse. All the kids would pretend, and go along with the story, but they were familiar with cigarette burns.

“I’m not sure, Ruthie.” Mark took her hand; it was cold and clammy. “But whatever it is, I’ll be okay. The most important thing is that you don’t say anything.” He was staring into her big doe eyes. “Not a peep, not a sound. If you need to cry, put your fist in your mouth.”

Ruthanne thought that was funny, trying to stuff her fist in her mouth. She almost tried it right then and there, but didn’t.

“I’m serious,” he said, looking back at the sound of approaching footsteps. His heart was racing, and the warmth of the hives was getting worse. The itch was almost intolerable, and when his punishment was done, he’d need to check if he had any leftover steroids to knock down the rash.

Conrad walked into the kitchen. His eyes went to his children, who were holding hands.

Mark let Ruthanne's hand fall, almost pushing her away. He was a smart boy, with a smart fucking mouth. He didn't want his father's attention on sweet Ruthanne.

"I was wracking my brain, thinking of a way to get my point across, Mark." Conrad tapped on his head like he was a philosopher. "And then it dawned on me, that smart fucking mouth of yours got you into this mess, it could get you out of it." He took a pair of nail clippers from his pocket.

Mark went cold.

To most people, the large set of clippers would be harmless; a basic grooming tool to manage their talons. Not to Conrad Haag. They were a tool of torture, something small and nasty that could help a disrespectful son see the error of his ways.

Conrad looked at the big clippers and gave them a couple of test clicks. Still worked. "Alright, boy, open your mouth."

Whenever Conrad was about to dish out a rather heinous punishment, his kids seemed to lose their names. They were no longer Ruthanne or Mark, but boy or girl.

Mark thought about fighting. He was nearly sixteen and had been doing farm work his entire life. He was thin, but strong, and had been in a few scraps here and there. But fighting his father? He didn't think he had it in him. Sure, he might get a lucky shot or two, but what then? He would have to leave home and never come back. Mark couldn't leave Ruthanne alone with him, at least not when she was so young. His mind raced with options, the last seeming as futile as the first. He settled on the easiest one: begging.

"Dad, please. I'm sorry for whatever I did, honest." He was starting to cry. If the boys at school saw him blubbering like a pussy, he'd never hear the end of it. But, it was genuine. He was shit scared and didn't deserve what was about to happen.

"Now hush," Conrad said, crossing the few steps in the kitchen to stand in front of his son. "You're crying like a big ole baby. When I was a boy, if I cried in front of my Pa, my punishment would've been even worse, you can bet your ass on that. Now, open your mouth." Conrad's face was red, and his brow was damp.

Mark's tears flowed unrestricted, and Ruthanne was silently weeping next to him. He didn't want to look for fear of turning his father's attention to her. With a quivering lip and shaking jaw, Mark opened his mouth.

Conrad looked into his boy's mouth, that disrespectful mouth. "Stick out your tongue," he ordered.

"Please, Dad—" Mark began.

Conrad was fast, slapping his son in the face, cutting off his begging.

The slap silenced everyone. Even the bugs seemed to stop their noises. The only sound still hanging in the air was flesh on flesh.

Conrad was seething, having such a pussy for a son. “If you don’t stop your bitching and open your fucking mouth, I’m going to move on and give Ruthanne your punishment.” He looked at his daughter, who recoiled away from him.

She choked out a loud cry and quickly silenced herself.

“Now, you wouldn’t want that, would ya?” Conrad was grinning, looking back at Mark.

Mark’s fear was turning to anger. He was concerned about his safety, that was true, but Ruthanne being hurt for him? No. That was unacceptable. “Fine,” Mark said, sticking out his tongue. “Get it over with.”

“Oh, thank you for the permission,” Conrad said, moving the clippers to his son’s mouth.

The cold steel couldn’t get too much meat, but it had more than enough. Conrad’s nostrils flared with anticipation as he wiggled the blades to get as much purchase on the tongue as possible. With a pinch, he clipped off the tip of his son’s tongue.

“Mmm, fuck,” Mark grunted. He sucked his tongue back into his mouth as it filled with blood; just moving it brought more agony. He put his hands to his mouth, as if covering it would stifle the pain. It did not.

Conrad looked at the clippers, the big nasty things he used on his infected toe nails. A little pink chunk of flesh was stuck in the blades with just a tiny drop of blood, hardly a punishment. He walked over to the sink and rinsed the meat from his clippers, then grabbed a cup from the drying rack and filled it with water. "Here," he said, handing the cup to Mark. "Rinse and spit."

His son looked up at him, fresh tears of pain welling up in the boy's eyes.

"We're not done."

Mark nearly lost his composure and screamed, but the pain in his tongue would be too much. *Not fucking done,* he thought, willing his tongue to stop bleeding. If he swallowed too much blood, he'd puke.

What the fuck else is he going to do to me? Mark took the glass and gulped. The water, even just tap water, burned his wound, but it was nice to rinse some of the blood. He swished it around like he did at the dentist that one time when he was Ruthanne's age. Conrad didn't give him another glass to spit in, and he didn't want to get up and spit in the sink. Mark only had the cup in his hand, which was better than nothing, and seemingly his only option. He drooled the bloody water into the glass. Swirls of crimson, saliva, and a little bit of tissue made a macabre scene in the cup.

Conrad snatched it from his son's hand, sloshing bloody water on the kitchen floor. "Okay, last thing and then you're free," he said, holding his freshly-cleaned nail clippers. "Open back up."

Mark was shaking. Not only from the pain in his already injured mouth, but the fact that he had no idea what else his father was thinking. His stomach cramped and a brutal wave of nausea pulled at his guts. Mark wondered, for a moment, if he puked on himself or his father, would this end? Would his dad show mercy and let him clean up? Or would the sick bastard make him sit in his vomit and take his medicine? He took a deep breath, keeping his gorge down for the time being. It was better to get it done and over with, no matter what the punishment entailed. With a last deep breath, he opened his mouth.

"Jesus H. Christ, you actually listened on the first time," Conrad said, smiling. "Now you're learning that crying like a fucking pussy won't do a damn thing. Not in this house and sure as fuck not in the real world." He grabbed his son's forehead and tilted his head back.

Trying not to gag as blood ran down his throat, Mark did his best to swallow with his mouth open. He looked his father in the eyes to show him he wasn't scared, but in reality, he was terrified, and Conrad knew it.

Conrad's nose twitched as if he smelled something unpleasant. He brought the clippers up, spreading the blades as wide as they would go. "Now, I've never done this, so bear with me." Gently, as if he cared, he put the clippers on one of Mark's incisors.

Mark began gulping air. The click of cold steel against his tooth was almost too much, let alone the fact of what was coming. He grabbed the edges of the chair and squeezed. He thought about

Ruthanne, who was still doing her best to keep her crying quiet. She was a good girl. Mark couldn't look at his father anymore. He squeezed his eyes shut as hard as possible, until he saw red.

"Okay, now hold still," Conrad said. He took his hand off Mark's forehead and gripped the nail clippers with both hands. Cutting through flesh was easy; he'd done that before. But he'd never cut through tooth or bone. He began to squeeze.

The pressure in Mark's tooth was unbearable. The blades were cutting, but it wasn't quick or clean. Every bit of pressure cracked and groaned, creasing the tooth further. Then, there was a sharp *click* sound as the blades came together.

When Mark was ten, he fell riding his bike and broke his arm. That was the worst pain he'd ever experienced in his short life. He thought he was going to die, and when he saw the bone poking from his skin, he was sure he was a goner. That pain was a match compared to a bonfire next to this.

The nail clippers cut the tooth clean in half, exposing the pulp and nerve to air for the first time. The little piece of tooth rocketed down Mark's throat, causing him to gag.

"There. Now we're done," Conrad said as he folded up the nail clippers and stuck them in his pocket. He wiped errant drool from his chin and left the room.

Mark's hands went back to his mouth. His eyes were still closed and squeezed hard. The pain in his tooth pulsed with every heartbeat. Each beat was agony like he'd never felt, like a fresh cut every time. The nausea was back, and with it came dizziness. He opened his eyes to a kitchen that looked like it was at sea. Everything was moving and there was a persistent ringing in his ears.

Ruthanne was standing in front of him, talking, but Mark couldn't hear a thing, just the ringing. Between the pain and blood, he was losing the fight with his stomach. There was no more keeping it down. In his last desperate move, he jumped out of the chair, pushing Ruthanne out of the way.

She stumbled, but didn't fall, and watched her brother run to the sink.

He braced himself on the counter, hoping he'd puke before passing out. The edges of his vision were turning black and, finally, his stomach gave in to the torment. A gush of vomit, which was mostly blood, burped from his mouth into the sink. He even saw the little chunk of his tooth riding the wave of gore as blackness enveloped him. He fell to the ground with those eight fucking words playing over and over in his head.

I don't like the cut of your jib.

Mark's world went black.

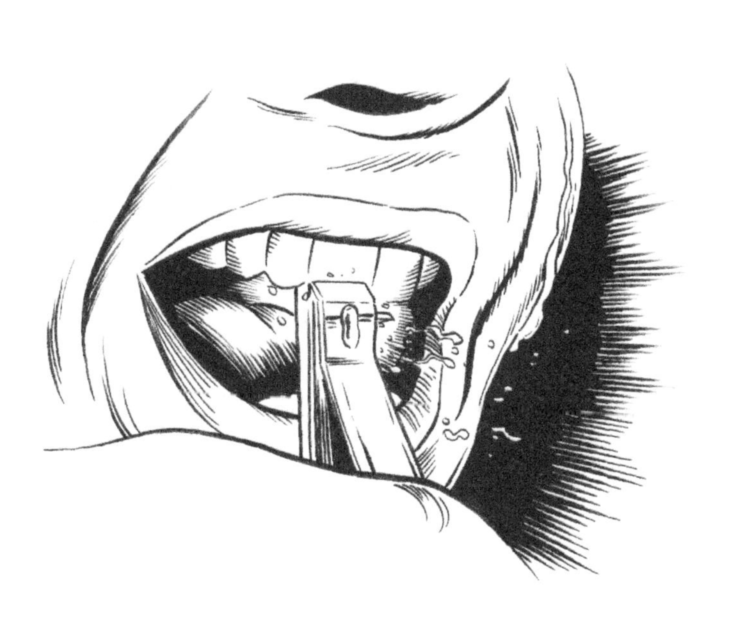

Mark jiggled the key in his apartment door. The lock was a pain in the ass, but his landlord refused to replace it. He told Mark it was fine and still locked. It didn't matter that it took almost half a minute to figure out the correct number of jiggles to get the tumblers to line up.

Finally, he got it, opening the door into his little studio.

It had been six years since the incident with his father and the nail clippers. His tooth was capped and repaired, thanks to a buddy in college who was learning to be a dental hygienist.

Mark tossed his keys on the little coffee table in front of his loveseat. It was a second, or possibly third-hand, couch, but it was perfect for him. He shuffled through the mail, which had nothing of interest, not even a bill, which was fine by him.

After he left home and headed to a state school, things began looking up. He was able to secure a sizeable amount of financial aid, and didn't have to bury himself in student loans. A few were needed, but that was to be expected. He graduated on time, unlike many students, and did it alone. He called home to let his father know, but the old man must've had better things to do, because he never showed at the ceremony. Mark didn't care; he hoped his father wouldn't show, but he missed Ruthie. She was fourteen, and growing into a woman. He talked to her a few times since leaving, but she didn't have a cellphone, and their father was always monitoring her calls.

Mark was able to land a small, paid internship, plus part-time work at a pizza place. He made more than enough to hold down his apartment and ate all the free pizza he could stomach. Life on the farm had kept him lean, but college life softened him a little. He still had his whip-like thinness, but a little belly poked out. He didn't mind, and the girls he met didn't mind either.

Just as he was about to heat up some cold pizza, his cellphone rang. He pulled it from his pocket and saw that it was home.

Ruthie, he thought, smiling. It was funny how a thought could almost summon someone.

"Hello," he said, waiting to hear his sister's voice on the other end. What he got was far from Ruthie, and the last person he wanted to talk to.

"It's me," Conrad said, his voice sounding like he'd eaten a fistful of gravel. He sniffled and Mark could picture him wiping his nose with the back of his hand.

"Dad?" Mark asked, as if it would be anyone else. "Where's Ruthie?" Mark's heart was pounding; something was wrong. His father never called him.

"Ruthanne is dead, Mark. She fell off the roof. The funeral is tomorrow. Come home, son."

That was it. That was all he said. No fucking explanation, no story. Hell, he didn't even call when she died, just to let him know the fucking funeral was the next day. The next fucking day.

Mark's mind was racing. He didn't want to believe it. It couldn't be real. His Ruthie? His little red-head sister, with the too big teeth? The girl who was going to escape the hell he'd left her in and go to New York and act? No, not his Ruthie. It had to be someone else.

"Mark!" Conrad barked into the phone. "Did you hear me? Your sister is dead."

Mark felt disembodied, like a ghost watching the conversation.

"Yeah, I heard you," he said, feeling like he was talking through someone else's mouth. "I'll be there."

"Okay, son. I'll see—"

He hung up on his father and tossed his phone on the loveseat. He stumbled over and collapsed, just missing his phone. The tears came hot and heavy and he tried to stem them with his fists. Tears of mourning poured from him, but that wasn't all. There was guilt—the guilt of leaving her with their piece of shit father. The guilt of leaving her in a loveless house working the farm. He cried hard and long. When he felt like he had no more tears, he called the bus company and bought a ticket.

Mark was going home.

***

The sun was shining and the weather was perfect. It would've been an ideal day, a day for old jeans and a soft t-shirt, and maybe a few beers. For Mark, it was far from perfect. It was the day they were burying his sister—the sister he left behind.

St. John's Church was filled to bursting, although that didn't mean much. The church only had room for 100 or so people, if that, and on a Sunday, they'd be lucky to get thirty. Not for Ruthie. For Ruthanne Haag, the church was packed. There were even people standing outside, kids mostly.

Like a zombie, Mark sat in the front pew next to his father, who stunk of English Leather and cigarettes. His suit was a few sizes too small, and his belt was digging into his little gut. It didn't matter. Nothing mattered. Mark stared with red, watery eyes at the casket in front of him. It was open, and he didn't know how he felt about that. He supposed most of the damage happened to the back of Ruthanne's head, but he didn't check.

Ruthanne lay there like an angel. The funeral director was wasting their talent in his small town, because they had a gift. Other funerals Mark had attended weren't so well done. The deceased looked like a wax figure, with their skin sallow and stretched. No, Ruthie, his Ruthie, looked like she was taking a nap. Her red hair was shimmering in the sunlight that crept in through the stained glass. Even the hue of her skin made her look alive.

Any second she'll wake up and yell 'surprise' and everyone will laugh at me. The insidious thoughts burrowed into Mark's brain. The thoughts that she wasn't dead and this was all a big fucking joke. *Ha-ha-ha, Mark, joke's on you.*

Mark heard a laugh to his right and turned to see his father hugging a bear of a man.

Conrad tried wrapping his arms around the big man, but failed. Instead, he patted him on the sides, exchanging laughs and a gentle ribbing.

Mark took a deep breath, the odor of his father wafting into his nostrils. He began to stand, ready to tell him this wasn't a fucking party, but a funeral for his fucking daughter who died on his watch. Mark stood just as the church organ began to play, signaling the beginning of the ceremony.

The rest of the church rose as the pastor and his small group of servers walked towards the altar.

Mark watched his father shake hands with the man one last time before directing his attention to the procession.

The pastor stood in front of Ruthanne's casket, raised his hands in silent prayer, and looked to the heavens. He lowered his arms and stared out at the sea of faces, most of which were tear streaked. "Please be seated," his baritone voice boomed.

The funeral for Ruthanne had begun.

***

Mark stood at Ruthanne's grave. It was freshly covered and stunk of earth. The sun was high in the sky, and the pleasant morning was turning into a warm day. His armpits and crotch were both a sweaty mess, but he didn't give a fuck.

He just stood there by that pile of dirt, the tons of earth covering his baby sister. He never heard the footsteps.

"I'm so sorry, Mark," a voice said from behind the grieving man.

Mark jumped and turned to see a sheriff's deputy standing near the headstone. It took Mark a moment, but the name finally clicked.

"Brandon? Is that you?" Mark asked, walking up to his old friend.

The deputy, a young man himself, smiled and looked at his polished boots.

"Yeah, it's me alright." He looked back up at Mark, grinning. "Nice getup, right?" He gestured to his uniform.

Mark, for the first time since getting the news about Ruthie, smiled. "Brandon Chance, Deputy Dog. Who would've guessed it?" Certainly not Mark, considering Brandon hadn't been the straightest arrow in high school.

"I know, right. Well, after you left, things took a turn for the worse. My mom, drunk as a skunk, lost control of her old Windstar." He was starting to tear up and brushed them away. "She hit a tree on County 1. Dead on arrival. I haven't had a drop since." He put his hands to his slender midsection, which was covered with body armor. "Did wonders for my girlish figure," he smirked. "Anyway, the reason I came over was just to give my condolences to you."

Mark nodded. "I appreciate that." He could tell there was something else on his friend's mind. "Something else, Brandon?"

The deputy, looking like a kid caught stealing, began to twist the toe of his boot in the earth. "Yeah," he said, leaving the growing divot alone. "I was first on scene for Ruthanne, Mark."

Mark felt the pain of the phone call coming back. That heart wrenching, gut churning fire, returning. He didn't stop the man from talking though.

"It was bad, Mark. Real bad."

Fresh tears slid down Mark's face. He didn't wipe them, only nodded.

"Your old man, though," he started nodding, ever so slightly, as if preparing his next statement, "he was just sitting there, next to her bod—I mean *her*— smoking a cigarette, listening to the radio. Not a fucking tear in his eye."

Mark had plenty of tears and they were flowing.

"Now, I'm not saying this isn't normal for some people. I've seen quite a few who've gone into shock. But Conrad Haag wasn't in shock. I'd bet my shield on that."

Mark didn't know why Brandon was telling him this. Maybe it was eating him up and he needed to get it off his chest. He wasn't sure, but he wasn't shocked.

"Anyway, I gotta get going." Brandon reached out to shake Mark's hand.

Mark took it and didn't resist when his friend pulled him in for a hug.

"Take care, Mark," Brandon said, as he released him. "We'll grab a bite next time you're in town. Hopefully on better conditions." Brandon turned and walked toward his waiting cruiser.

Mark saw his father sitting in his old truck.

"You ready?" Conrad yelled across the cemetery.

Mark stared at him and began walking through the grass, careful not to step on any graves.

***

Mark pushed the last bit of pizza crust into his mouth. He washed it down with a beer and decided he was going to finish the beer too, then set the empty bottle on the table next to half-dozen others.

Conrad, not to be outdone by his son, chugged his beer down and slammed it on the table. The other bottles rattled, and he let out a deep burp. "Ah, that was good," he said, wiping errant suds from his chin. He actually shaved for the funeral, which was a shock.

The night hadn't been terrible, at least after the funeral. Mark and his father grabbed a pizza and a couple of twelve packs. They sat at the old table, almost the exact spot where Conrad mutilated his son with the nail clippers, and had dinner. They shared stories about Annie, Conrad's wife and his and Ruthanne's mother. They spoke of happier times—times when they were a family, not just a group of strangers trying to make ends meet. Then, they switched to Ruthanne. They talked, drank, and ate until the pizza was gone. The beer wasn't gone, though, there was always plenty of that in their house.

Conrad reached into the twelve pack and came out empty. "Damn," he said, shaking the box as if a beer would materialize. "Go out in the garage and grab another out of the fridge, would'ya," he said to his son.

Mark was feeling pretty good. He wasn't drunk, but had a nice buzz going. He knew he'd regret it in the morning, especially if they got into another twelve pack, but he didn't give a fuck. He was going to drink the pain away. "Sure thing, Pops," he said, getting out of his chair and walking towards the attached garage.

Ever since Mark was a boy, the garage never changed. It was small, almost too small for a car, but it didn't matter. There was too much shit piled in there for a car to be parked anyway. The garage was typical: work bench, peg board with tools, random farm equipment, and car parts. And of course, the fridge. An ancient relic to the days when appliances were built to last. The thing still ran cold and would probably outlive them all.

Mark opened the fridge and grabbed a fresh twelve pack. An empty six pack was sitting there, and he pulled that out too. He tossed the empty into the garbage can next to the fridge.

"What the hell?" Mark said to himself as he looked in the garbage can.

The handle of a hammer, his father's roofing hammer, was poking out from a pile of paper towels.

Mark reached into the can and grabbed it.

It was a mess. The head of the tool was covered in dried blood. Flakes of it were peeling off, but there was quite a bit of it. Mark was shuddering as his eye caught something else in the fluorescent lighting. He put the twelve pack down, not taking his eyes off the hammer. Gently, ever so gently, he plucked a red hair from the bloody mess of the hammer face. Ruthie's hair.

He squeezed the handle so tight he felt like his knuckles would burst. He guessed his father didn't like the cut of Ruthie's jib.

Mark walked back into the house, his heart was racing and pounding so hard he thought he might pass out.

Conrad sat at the table drinking the asses of all the empties. He never heard his son walk in.

Mark looked at the balding head of his father, the man who was supposed to love and raise them, guide them to adulthood. No, he fucking snatched that from Ruthie. He picked a spot on his father's skull and swung. At the last second, Mark took a little off the swing. He didn't want to kill the old man, just have a little talk with him… and some power tools.

***

Conrad woke up with the worst headache of his life. Beer usually didn't hit him like that, but his brain felt like it was trying to escape. His eyes were still closed. He was afraid the light would pierce his eyeballs. Slowly, he started to come too, realizing a couple of peculiar things.

The first thing his battered brain computed was the fact he was naked. It wasn't the first time he'd gone to bed drunk and woken up naked, but the feeling of rough concrete, and the smell of motor oil, had him quite alarmed. Not only was he naked, but he was in the garage…duct taped to a chair.

Gently, Conrad opened his eyes. The fluorescent light assaulted him, making him wince in pain. He tried to turn his head away from the offending glow, but couldn't. His head had also been secured to the chair. Blinking, he allowed his eyes to adjust and pushed away the pain. He needed answers and he fucking needed them immediately.

"Hey," he croaked. His mouth was dry and tasted like cat shit. Conrad moved his tongue around, trying to gather a little saliva. He wet his lips and called out again. "Hey, you cocksucker! Let me the fuck out of here!" He wasn't quite sure who he was yelling at, but he had a good idea.

The garage door, the one leading to the house, opened. Mark stood in the threshold. His dress shirt was disheveled, and he was sweaty. He had a pissed off look on his face.

"Finally awake." He stepped into the garage, closing the door behind him. He had something behind his back, but Conrad couldn't see. "Good. I thought I killed you. Now, that would be a damn shame, wouldn't it, Pops?"

Conrad was starting to get his wherewithal back and began pulling at the bonds. His wrists, ankles, head, and waist had been wrapped tight in duct tape. He figured Mark used a whole damn roll on him. Sweat ran down his body. Not the sweat of a hard day's work, but the perspiration of fear.

Mark took the hammer from behind his back and looked at it. He stared at the red hair and flakes of blood on the face of the head. "What did she do?" he asked, not looking at his father. Tears were filling his eyes, but he fought them back. "What the fuck could little Ruthie have done to you to make you crack her in the fucking head with a hammer? On the fucking roof!"

Taking his eyes off the hammer, he glared at his father. He reached into his back pocket and pulled out a large plastic bag, put the hammer in, and sealed it up, then walked over to the tool bench and set it down. He picked up a drill.

Conrad tried to watch his son, but couldn't see him at the tool bench. He was braced for another blow to the head, and hoped it would kill him. When he heard the drill, a little squirt of piss shot from his withered cock.

Mark held the drill and gazed at the bit in it. It wasn't very large, but it would get the job done.

Besides, he didn't want his dear old dad to bleed out too quickly. He scanned the bench for something else. Luckily, his father was very organized. Mark picked up a pair of pliers. Now, he was ready for their little talk.

"Why did you do it, Dad?" Mark asked as he wheeled a stool over. He plopped down in front of his father, the tools in hand. "Why did you kill Ruthie?"

Conrad looked at his son. His chest felt like it was going to explode and he prayed for a heart attack, but it didn't come. He didn't speak, just stared, trying to intimidate the young man in front of him who inherited too many of his bad qualities.

"Oh, the silent treatment," Mark said. His grin widened. He set the tools on the floor and reached into his pocket. "Let me guess, you didn't like the cut of her jib? Huh, did she say something a little smart to you? Did she belittle you, you fucking slug? Is that why you hit her?" Mark unfolded the pair of nail clippers in front of his face. He gave them a couple of test clicks, just to make sure. "Well, Dad, my dear father, let's see if we can cut a little of your fucking jib."

Mark jumped off the stool and grabbed his father's head. He didn't have to hold it; the duct tape was taking care of that. He grabbed Conrad's right eyelid just before he could squeeze it shut. The left he'd have to work for, but the right, that was all his.

"What the fuck are you doing?" Conrad spat as he tried to close his eye.

Mark was pulling the skin up, tearing out every single lash. "Oh, I don't want you to miss a thing, so what better way than to take your eyelids off?" He slid the blade of the nail clipper under the flap of flesh.

The cold metal stung Conrad's eyeball, causing a flood of tears.

"I didn't fucking kill Ruthanne, you crazy fuck!" Conrad was in desperation mode; he could feel the clippers getting tighter.

Mark squeezed. He wasn't expecting it to be so easy, but then he remembered the only things he ever clipped were nails. A thin piece of flesh was nothing.

Conrad screamed and tears of blood ran down his face.

The whole eyelid didn't come off in one shot. Mark readjusted, getting more flesh in between the blades, and snipped again. More blood, more screaming. Divine.

"Motherfucking cocksucker!" Conrad spat. He looked insane with one bare eyeball.

Well, Mark was going to do him a favor and even them out. "Open the other eye," Mark said. There was no asking at that point. He was well beyond that.

"Fuck you," Conrad spat a thick loogie at his son, missing him.

Mark smiled again. "Perfect," he said as he picked up the pliers. He thought about ripping the eyelid off, but he liked options.

Conrad saw the pliers and figured his son was just going to force the eye open. When he felt the cold steel wrapping around his balls, he almost pissed again.

"Now, Dad, you have two options. The first is you open your eye and let me do a little light grooming. Or, I crush your miserable nuts one at a time." He put a little pressure on the pliers, feeling them squeeze the delicate organs. "Your choice."

Conrad felt like puking. The pain in his testicles was already intense, and he knew Mark was barely touching them. Reluctantly, he opened his eye.

"Wonderful," Mark said, dropping the pliers. "Now, hold still, this will only take a second." He shoved the nail clippers deep under his father's eyelid and snipped.

Conrad didn't scream as the whole thing was taken off in one clip. Blood ran down his face, wetting the thin layer of stubble.

"Great, now we can begin." Mark folded up the nail clippers and stuck them back in his pocket. "Why'd you kill Ruthie?"

"Fuck you," Conrad said, his eyes wide open. "I didn't. It was a fucking accident." Even after seeing the hammer, he was still sticking with his story.

Mark picked up the drill. He put the bit to Conrad's knee. "Last chance."

Conrad spat again, hitting Mark in the face.

Mark didn't flinch or even wipe it; he just pulled the trigger on the drill.

The bit made short work of the flesh, seeking hard bone beneath. The knee cap was a resilient little bastard, but Mark put some weight behind the drill. The bit hissed and bogged down as it bore through. It did a great job of drowning out Conrad's screams. The smell of meat and bone dust permeated the air.

Reversing the direction of the drill bit, Mark backed it out. The tight grooves were full of gore, with ribbons of flesh hanging like streamers. Chips of bone were strewn in with the red. Conrad was screaming, but Mark didn't care; he had work to do.

The drill bit was warm from the friction, but it was about to be an inferno. Mark stood and put the bit higher, just at the middle of the femur. He pulled the trigger and plunged it into his father's thigh. There was much more meat to get through, but the drill did what it needed to do. Conrad's femur was tougher than his kneecap and Mark didn't know if the little bit would make it. It did, biting through the bone and into the marrow.

Conrad's screams went unheard. The pain was unbearable and he felt sick. He burped once, and then again, the second one unleashing a splash of beer and pizza vomit.

Mark looked at his father, covered in his own puke and whimpering. Pathetic. He took his medicine better than this when his dad went at him with the nail clippers, and he was just a teenager. He hoped his dear, old father had a little left in him, because it was far from over.

"You little fuck!" Conrad shouted. "When I get free, I'm gonna fucking cut your nuts off! You hear me? Huh, you little pussy!"

Mark heard him, but didn't care. He was busy looking at all the wonderful tools hanging up. His careful eye settled on one. He picked it up, checked to ensure it was in proper working condition, and walked back in front of his father.

Conrad's breathing was starting to settle. He was getting a grip on the pain, willing it away as best he could. When he saw Mark with the tin snips, he almost cried. The drill wounds were bad, and plenty painful, but would heal. Whatever Mark was planning on doing with the snips, he didn't want to know.

"You know, Conrad. I just don't think I can call you Dad anymore. A father is a man who cherishes and cares for their family, not one who tortures and kills."

Conrad stared at his son, not that he could do much else without eyelids. His eyes were burning in his skull and his body was screaming for him to blink.

"I just don't like the cut of your jib, Conrad," Mark said, stepping closer. He leaned down, face-to-face with the man he once called *Dad*. "So, let's see what we can cut off. Maybe then I'll like you." Mark smiled. The sweet farm boy was gone. He opened the tin snips and grabbed Conrad's hand.

Instinct kicked in and the older man made a tight fist, hiding his fingers from his demented son.

"Now, Conrad," Mark said, trying to pry his father's fist open. "I'm just going to take the pinky at the first knuckle. Just a little snip and that's it." He kept pulling, but the old man had a grip like iron. Mark stopped and decided he'd change tactics. "Okay, since you're being a pussy, I'll cut elsewhere." He thought about cutting his cock and balls off, but no part of him wanted to touch that shriveled thing.

The little toe. that would do nicely.

Mark knelt down and grabbed Conrad's foot. There was no hiding those little piggies.

"Fucking stop, alright!" Conrad begged. "I'll tell them I did it. Call the police and I'll give a full confession. Just please, put the snips down." Conrad's chest was heaving. He'd never had a heart attack, but a tightness was crushing his chest.

Mark wiggled the blades around the toe and squeezed. The old tin snips were sharper than he thought. They made short work of the little bone, taking it off in a clean cut.

Conrad screamed and thrashed, but Mark wasn't done. One by one, he cut the rest of Conrad's toes off. The big toe gave him a bit of a struggle, but with a little elbow grease, he got through it.

Mark stood up. He was drenched in sweat, but felt great. He felt like justice, his justice, justice for Ruthie, was almost complete.

Conrad was in agony. Blood flowed from the stumps of his missing digits, mixing with some chunks of vomit.

Mark pulled his cellphone from his pocket and blocked his number. He didn't know if it would work with the sheriff's office phones, but he didn't really give a fuck. He dialed the number.

"Thank you, son. Please, get me help. I need a hospital." Conrad grimaced. "I think I'm having a heart attack."

"Fuck you," Mark said as he listened to the phone ring. A familiar voice answered on the other end.

"Sheriff's office, this is Deputy Chance. How may I help you?" Brandon said.

Mark didn't think he'd get away with the things he'd done to his father, but his old friend hearing his voice didn't help much. Hopefully he sounded different on the phone and Brandon didn't remember their little encounter at the cemetery. He didn't even know what to say, so he just blurted something out.

"Murder. 215 Regliche Road." Mark hung up. His heart was thumping and he knew his time was limited. There was one last thing to take care of.

Conrad was in pain. The torture throbbed; his wounds wept blood and plasma. The real pain came from his heart. No, it wasn't his heart hurting for the death of his daughter, or the years of abuse he'd inflicted on his son. It was a heart attack. Not a major one, but it sure hurt like hell.

"Mark, my boy," he said as his son walked behind him. Sweat was pouring down Conrad's face at a steady pace. A few errant drops stung his eyes as he tried to blink them away. "Please, this is over. I'm dying anyway, just leave me be," he pleaded. Another twist in his heart and his sight went fuzzy. The pain lingered and squeezed until it let up, restoring his vision. Mark stood in front of him.

"You keep saying your heart hurts, your heart hurts." Mark was crying. Crying for Ruthie, crying for the death of his loving mother, but mostly crying for the death of the young boy he once was, the little boy his father killed with neglect and abuse. "What fucking heart?" Mark yelled, spit hitting Conrad in the face. "Well, let's see if you do have one." He lifted the Phillips head screwdriver and placed the tip against his father's bare chest.

Conrad looked at the tool dimpling his skin. He didn't think his body could take any more abuse. "Please." It was the only thing he could mutter. Strings of spit clung to his lips.

Mark put pressure on the handle, feeling the tip pierce flesh.

Conrad barely fought it, just a little wiggle, but that was it.

Mark looked him in the eyes as the screwdriver made it through the layer of muscle and hit bone. He shifted the tip, moving it up and down, hoping to find a space between the ribs. He did. The steel invaded the cavity, seeking the pounding organ.

Conrad mouthed *please* again, but there was no sound.

Mark pushed and felt the pulse of his father's unloving heart. This was it. The end of his torment. "Well Conrad, this is for Ruthie, and for me." Mark thrust, feeling the panic of the heart as a perverse object penetrated it. "We didn't like the cut of your jib either." Mark kept pushing and pushing.

Blood dribbled from Conrad's mouth and dripped down his chin like a movie effect, but it was real.

The screwdriver finally stopped when the handle met bone.

Staring into his father's dead eyes, Mark thought, *Were they ever alive? Was there ever any love in them?* He didn't have too much time to ponder as the sound of approaching sirens caught his attention.

Mark left the grisly remains leaking blood and cooling in the garage. He grabbed the hammer, the one used to murder Ruthie, and put it on Conrad's lap. That should help with the investigation and put his sister's spirit to rest. Then, he grabbed the keys to the old farm truck and went outside.

The night was cool and full of stars. It was one of those nights he and Ruthie would've liked to sit outside and sip sweet tea and just stare at the sky.

The old truck turned over with a growl and puff of smoke. Mark guided it out of the driveway and onto the road. The cherry lights of the sheriff's cars lit up the night, but he drove right past them. He didn't have a plan, and he knew they'd come looking for him.

In the sky a star twinkled, one brighter than the others.

"Ruthie," he said, a smile on his face. Mark aimed the nose of the truck towards the star, and drove.

GREEN BLEEDS RED

I realize most people don't watch porn while munching on popcorn and drinking beer, but that's exactly what I was doing when Libby—who died three fucking years ago—knocked on the door.

"Who the fuck is that?" I muttered.

The scene was just getting good, and I was as hard as a rock. I was gonna stroke it after I finished my popcorn, but some asshole was knocking. I had to remember to wash my hands first. Last time I jerked off with popcorn fingers, my cock was on fire from the delicious salt.

I paused the video on the good ole smart TV. My favorite porn star, Killer Bunny, was just about to turn over and take it up the ass. I loved her videos, and of course, she was hot, a brunette; Libby was a blonde, covered in tattoos. There wasn't much that was off limits for Killer Bunny, unlike Libby, who would never take it up the ass.

I pushed the bowl of popcorn, which was mostly kernels, off my lap.

"I'm coming," I yelled to the nagging fuck, who was still knocking.

It was probably some religious asshole, or someone selling trash, neither of which I was interested in. I just wanted to dismiss them and get a good jerk in.

I adjusted my erection, tucking it into the waistband of my sweatpants, a move that boys had been doing since we had waistbands. My helmet poked out a little. What could I say, God gave me a gift. I covered it with my shirt, thankful it was black so no pre-cum marked it.

I unlocked the door and prepared to tell whoever it was to fuck off. I threw the door open and nearly shit my pants when I saw Libby standing there.

"Ricky," she moaned.

I stood dumbfounded, staring at my dead wife. Well, I guess she wasn't quite dead and, in my heart, I knew she wasn't.

The last time I'd seen Libby was three years ago. She and I were more outgoing than I was alone, and we had a lifetime of adventures lined up. The first of many was some rustic camping. It was supposed to be perfect, and it started that way. I did lots of research, mapped out our course, and stocked up on supplies. Before I knew it, we were hiking through the Adirondacks. The mountains were beautiful, but not as beautiful as my Libby. At night and sometimes in the day, we would have wild sex. It was one of the few times in our short marriage where Libby wasn't too prudish. I couldn't fuck her ass, but just about everything else was fair game.

Then, one night, she went out to pee and vanished. Not a sound, not a scream or a peep, just vanished.

I, the loving husband I was, fell back asleep just after she'd zippered up the tent. I didn't realize something was wrong until the sun was up. I panicked, screaming her name until my throat was raw. The rescuers came in droves, with dogs and even a helicopter, but Libby was lost, or so I thought.

"Libby?" I asked, as if it could be anyone else.

It was her, just as I remembered. She was wearing the same clothes: a pair of fleece pajama pants and my old Slipknot t-shirt. That shirt had seen better days, but she loved it even as the material was getting thin. I noticed something else, something immediate: a scent. Libby smelled like the woods. Even a couple feet away, I could smell the earth on her. It wasn't a bad smell, but it was odd. I guess it shouldn't have been, considering she'd been lost for three years.

Libby smiled at me, that cute little upturned corner of her mouth smile, the one that drove me wild. She brushed an errant strand of blonde hair behind an ear and laughed. "Uh, yeah, who else would it be?"

Yes, I guess my question was quite dumb, but I was thoroughly in shock. There, standing in front of me, seemingly unscathed, was my wife. My wife, who went missing in one of the most unforgiving mountain ranges in the Northeast. My wife, who was wearing the same clothing as the night she went missing.

And there I was with popcorn fingers and a hard-on. Welcome home, dear.

My racing mind finally caught up with the fact she was home. My Libby had come back to me.

At that moment, I didn't care how or why, just that she was back.

"Can I come in?" she asked, which was a pretty dumb question considering it was her house too.

That was enough for me. I felt my sanity and emotions wearing down and cracking. Tears were starting to burn my eyes and I opened my arms for her.

"Libby," I croaked through a healthy glob of phlegm that had found its way into my throat. She lurched forward into my arms, and wrapped hers around me.

"I thought you were gone forever," I said, breathing in the mossy undertones of her hair. I hugged her so tight, so damn tight, I thought I was going to break her, but no. She had the same, healthy, curvy body as the last time I saw her. Now, I knew that wasn't the time, but I had very limited female contact over those three years.

When Libby went missing, I did everything I could to find her. After the police and firefighters had exhausted their options, I found others. I hired private guides, woodsman, hunters, even a fucking medium, to find my Libby. All the while I focused on that, not my love life. Deep down, I knew she was alive somewhere.

It took a while to bring myself to seek another female companion. Almost one year to the day, I did just that. I'm not proud of myself, but I had a quick fuck with a barfly in my car. It was hot, somewhat uncomfortable, and gross. My car smelled like raunchy ass for a few days after that encounter. I was so disgusted with myself, and had such deep regret, I nearly swore off women all together. Well, that didn't happen, but from then on, I only fucked around at illicit massage parlors. Yes, I had to pay for a handjob, which was all I ever got, but it was better than nothing. After a few awkward, silent handjobs by women who could barely speak English, I gave up on them too. Just my hand from then on, sans the popcorn fingers.

"Oh, Ricky," Libby loosened her embrace, which was just as tight as mine, and looked at me face to face.

I looked like shit and probably had a nice combo of beer and popcorn breath, but she didn't seem to care.

"I missed you," she said.

Her breath, unlike mine, was sweet smelling, almost like she'd been eating pine needles.

"I missed you too, Libs. I missed you too," I told her, as her lips began closing in on mine.

Let me tell you, I've never been so excited for a kiss since my first one, when I was twelve, with Brittany Lacey behind the elementary school.

Libby's lips were warm on mine, and felt oh so soft. The pine undertones of her breath mingled with mine, our tongues finding each other.

My cock felt like it was going to burst, not cum, but explode from how fucking hard it was.

Her stomach was pressed tight against mine and grinding against my swollen dick.

Libby pushed me into the house, kicking the door shut with a heavy slam.

I had so many fucking questions, but my male DNA was overriding any sense I had.

Libby was in control as she drove me into the house. Our mouths had yet to come unlocked, and were just a flurry of spit and teeth smashing together. Her breasts pressed against me and I could feel the hardness of her small nipples through my shirt.

The couch slammed into the back of my legs, tripping me. I fell, just missing the popcorn bowl, which went flying from the weight of us hitting the cushion.

"I need you, Ricky," Libby said, finally coming up for air. "I need your seed inside of me." She ripped her shirt off, baring those awesome tits I'd missed so much.

Wait a minute, did she just ask for my *seed*? And inside of her? I'm not one to turn down such a request, but even in my lust, I paused. During our dating and marriage, I rarely—and I mean rarely—came inside of Libby. This was for a couple of reasons. The first of which was that she wasn't on any kind of birth control. No pills, patches, or shots. She couldn't stand what the hormones did to her body, and she was afraid of blood clots. She tried the IED or IUD, whatever it was, for a while, but even that made her nervous. Second was the fact she hated the feel of condoms, as did I, so those were scrapped after a couple of fuck sessions. The third was that she didn't like the feeling of cum inside of her. She hated leaking the next day, the constant feeling of something dripping from her. I have to say, it didn't sound too comfortable. Me, being the gentleman I was, would oblige her and shoot my spunk on her stomach (usually right in the belly button, which would always make her laugh) or across her back. Either way was fine, as long as it came out of me. Now, you see why her asking for a hot shot in the ole puss was odd.

My pause was short as she ground her pussy against my raging erection. If she kept that up, my seed would be in my sweats.

Libby thrusted a tit into my face. I sucked her nipple, which was rock hard, into my waiting mouth. She dug her fingers into my hair, scratching my scalp and moaning.

"I need you, now," she breathed into my ear.

Her lips tickled me. The heat coming from her crotch felt like an inferno.

Libby slid off me and pulled her pajama pants down. Even her pussy looked the same, with just a slight layer of stubble from shaving in the woods.

I couldn't help but stare at the naked goddess in front of me. Libby was the vision of beauty and she was almost glowing with sexuality. I know that sounds odd, and it could be the fact I hadn't busted a nut in anything besides my hand in years, but damn she looked amazing. My eyes were just darting all over her nudity and I noticed a small drop of glistening wetness slipping from her pussy.

"Are you going to take your pants off, or would you like me to?" Libby asked, the side-smile making another appearance.

In my stupor, I forgot to free my aching penis, which had left a massive wet spot of pre-cum on my sweats. I've never taken pants off as fast as then. My dick was barely free when Libby jumped back on me.

There was no romance or preamble, just fucking.

Libby straddled me, locking our mouths back together. Her tongue shot between my lips and I sucked it…hard. Her free hand, the one not digging into my scalp, grabbed my cock and guided it to her awaiting cunt.

I could almost feel it calling to me, welcoming me home. My slick helmet passed between her soaked lips. Libby moaned into my mouth as she grazed the swollen nub of her clit with my cock. She pulled it away, and pushed it back towards her wetness…and took the whole thing.

I wanted to apologize to her, because I knew I would only last seconds. The feeling of being back inside of her was like heaven. Every stroke felt better than jerking off, and I could feel my body getting ready to unleash. I could also feel something else: Libby was working up an orgasm too. That wasn't odd, she'd get off a decent amount when we fucked, but never that fast.

"Holy shit!" she yelled, grinding hard against me.

I was at the point of no return and balls deep, so there would be no last-minute pull out here and I was a-ok with that.

We came together, a rarity, but always enjoyed.

"Fuck," I muttered, allowing my brain to process the chemical dump it was experiencing. Libby was still on me and I was still in her. The ebbs and flows of her orgasm were still pulsing and her breathing was rough in my ear. I could feel the thumping of her heart against mine, as I pulled her closer.

Without a word, she dismounted me, and cupped her leaking vagina. Naked, she ran to the bathroom.

I sat there, my cock still hard as a rock, and grabbed my discarded beer, which was on the end table. It was warm, but I didn't care. I chugged the rest, let out a little burp, and put my head back.

Post-nut clarity was what they called it, and by *they*, I mean me. It's the moments after you bust a nut that things come into focus. I had it after I banged that pig in the back of my car. I was all for it, hammering away on her smelly ass, until I came. Once the poison was out of me, my world came crashing back to reality. I felt like shit, like I'd cheated on Libby, which I guess I did, since she was back. I had so many questions and I was sure more would come as we sat down and talked.

The toilet flushed and my Libby came sauntering out. Her cheeks were red and her beautiful tits bounced in a way that drove me wild. A small drop of leftover cum peeked out of my dick. My little buddy liked what he saw too.

Libby plopped down next to me, still nude, and picked up my empty beer can.

"There's more in the fridge," I said, not even thinking that she might be starving. I jumped up to go grab her a beer. "I have some cold cuts, if you want a sandwich," I said, looking at the near-empty shelves.

"Just the beer is fine," Libby replied. "You filled me right up."

I smiled, grabbing the beer and walking back into the living room.

Libby was sitting with her legs crossed, but the way she was looking at me told me we weren't done for the day. But first, I had a few questions.

"Here you go," I said, handing her the beer.

She opened the tab and took a long drink. "Ah, that hits the spot," she said, setting it down next to my empty can. "You feel like hitting the spot again?" she asked, spreading her legs.

I did, I really did, but the totality of the craziness was actually overloading my sex drive. My hardon didn't agree, but my brain was winning for once. I knew we were gonna fuck again, so I was not trying to rush it. Maybe next time I would be able to hold out a little longer. Maybe.

"Libs," I said, sitting down next to her.

"Yes," she cooed, her finger tips touching my cock. It jumped at the gentle sensation and prospect of more fun.

I was becoming overwhelmed, not just by the sex, which was a nice treat. No, the fact my wife, who hadn't been seen in three years, was stroking my cock like nothing happened, was really getting to me. I'm not much of a crier, per se, but I could feel the tears building up. Libby, my Libby, was back.

"You're alive," I said, taking her fingers from my member. I placed her hand against my cheek, ignoring the fact she had a little cum on her finger tips. It was her, really her.

Libby giggled, almost like a child, and caressed my face. "Of course, I'm alive," she said to me, matter-of-factly.

I was never one to look a gift horse in the mouth, but this was too much, even for me. "We need to get you to a doctor, and…and," my mind was racing, "call your family. They've been a mess since you left. We even had a funeral for you." I chuckled at the thought of an empty casket and headstone for a woman who was very much alive.

Libby moved her hand from my cheek and put it on the back of my head. Her fingers played through my hair, which was a little longer than normal.

"Shh," she whispered, with a playful and lustful look in her eyes. "I'm fine. There's no need for a doctor." Libby thrusted her breasts towards me, which I was happy to look at. "Do I look like I need a doctor?"

I looked her up and down, my cock aching to be back inside of her. I felt a trail of slime run down my shaft.

"No, I guess not," I said, smiling at her. My curiosity outweighed my sex drive, for once. "But how?"

Libby took her hand off my head. I could still feel her on my scalp. She looked at me. "The Goddess. She and her children, they were the ones who sheltered me, who cared for me and saved me."

"The Goddess?" I asked, feeling like we were about to take a walk down a weird path. Libby didn't look hurt, and she certainly was healthy, but it seemed like a screw may have come loose when she was in the woods.

"Yes, the Goddess. She called to me, Ricky. She told me she could save me, could make me something so much more, but she wasn't well. She nurtured me, took care of me, but told me she needed my help." Libby looked away, staring at the corner of the ceiling. I followed her eyes, but only saw cobwebs. Within a second or two, she returned her stare to me. There were tears in her eyes, but she blinked them away. "I had to help her, Ricky. No matter what." Her hand absently went to her stomach, but only for a second, before moving down to her snatch.

I followed her fingertips as they disappeared inside of her. The squelch of wetness and look in her eyes was more than enough to push away any thoughts of some fucking Goddess. If I didn't cum again soon, my dick was going to explode.

Libby knew what she was doing to me, staring at me as her wet fingers caress the little nub of her clit. She stood up, her nudity on full display, and turned around.

"The Goddess wants more of you, Ricky," she said, getting on the couch, but facing away from me. Libby was on all fours, leaning her forearms on the arm of the couch. As lithe as a cat, she lowered her head and raised her ass into the air.

I was nearly beside myself. Her asshole and pussy were on full display. While examining her holes, something else caught my eye—a patch of moss. It wasn't much, but it was there, stuck right on her left butt cheek. I was going to brush it off, but I didn't want to embarrass her, especially if that knocked her out of the mood.

"The Goddess wants you to fuck me like an animal," she said, looking over her shoulder at me.

I smiled and knelt on the couch, lining myself up with her glistening slit. I wouldn't want to disappoint the Goddess, now, would I?

***

The shower felt great. The hot water sluiced the sex juice from my body, and let me tell you, there was plenty of it. After the bout on the couch, Libby was starving and I couldn't blame her. We ordered a pizza and ate the entire thing, along with polishing off the rest of my beer.

After our recharge meal, Libby showered, and I hoped some of the outdoors smell would come off her, but it didn't. It would probably take her a few more showers to get that smell off. It was like working in a gas station; that smell was always a part of you, at least for a little while.

I didn't have much hot water, but what was left felt amazing. It was starting to dwindle and I realized it was time to end my cleansing.

I dried and dressed and found Libby sitting on the couch, the same one we'd defiled not long ago, flipping through our wedding album. She was wearing a pair of shorts, one of her t-shirts, and clearly no bra.

"Anything good?" I asked, sitting next to her. I put my arm around her shoulders and played with an errant strand of her hair. It was still damp from the shower, but I didn't mind.

Libby closed the book and sat it on the end table. "Oh, yes. Everything is great," she said as she looked at me, her lips partially open.

I could see her wet tongue slithering around. She had that look of lust in her eyes again. Now, I'm not an old man, but I haven't fucked three times in a day since I was in my twenties. I felt myself stiffening, so I guess my body made that decision for me.

Libby grabbed my arm, the one around her shoulders, and kissed the inside of my wrist. She pulled my hand off her shoulders and kissed my palm. Without warning, she put my pointer finger into her mouth, and sucked it the same way she used to suck my cock.

I was full-blown hard. "Mmm," I moaned, "that brings back memories."

Libby looked me in the eyes and pulled my finger, wet with her saliva, from her mouth. "I'm sure it does," she said, guiding my hand to her crotch. She pulled her shorts to the side, revealing her nude vagina. She obviously wasn't a fan of any type of undergarment.

Gently, Libby slid my finger into her. The warmth and tightness were amazing. It was as if I hadn't fucked her twice already. I wasn't sure what had gotten into me, but I just wanted to keep fucking, to keep dropping loads in her until I died.

Libby began riding my finger, taking it in and out of her as her pussy juice wet her shorts.

"I want…your mouth," she said, pulling my finger from her.

I have no issue performing oral, and actually quite like it, so I smiled and got on the ground.

Libby was staring away again, as if she was listening to something I couldn't hear.

My mind was not on phantom sounds; it was on eating pussy, and that's what I was going to do. I reached up and grabbed the waistband of her shorts.

This broke her attention from whatever the fuck she was looking at or listening to.

Libby looked down at me and gave me a hungry smile.

I'm not the most seductive of men, but I do enjoy going down on my wife. It was one of the few things I felt I was genuinely good at. I gave her shorts a little tug, giving her the hint I couldn't start my feast with them on.

Libby lifted her ass as I pulled her shorts off. She spread her legs, putting herself on full display, and leaned back.

I smiled at her, and the beautiful thing in front of me, and got to work. Something was off. I know the human body has a variety of odors and tastes, and when I'm horny, none of them bother me. But this, this was different. Libby's pussy smelled like dirt. Not dirty like sweaty or smelling, but like fresh dirt. I looked at her slit, wondering if maybe she had a little on her, like the random moss on her ass. I didn't see anything and tried to push it away. In my brain, I was telling myself it was because she'd been in the woods for so long. That was the reason she had a general outdoors smell. Even though she just showered, it was lingering.

Forcing it from my mind, I did my best to satisfy my wife. I always started off by kissing her thigh, working my way down to the sweetness in the center.

"No," Libby said, stopping me in my tracks.

I looked up at her, my hands wrapped around her legs. “No?” I asked.

“I don’t need any warming up,” she said, with a grin on her face.

I gave her a smile and didn’t say a word. I figured if she was ready to cum, even better. I would finish her fast and see if she wanted to suck me off. We had pretty much hit every sexual position earlier, so why not get reacquainted with a good ole blow job.

I figured I’d just go for the crowd pleaser—lick her clit and finger her at the same time. That usually was my finishing move, and always worked.

As my face was nearing her pussy, the smell of earth grew stronger, like she had a hole in the ground between her legs. I pushed the thought away and started in on her. My fingers slid in without issue, and her little nub practically vibrated under my tongue. Libby was letting out the sweetest of moans, so I knew I was hitting all the spots. Then, I felt something move over my fingers.

“What the fuck?” I yelled, pulling my hand away with a slurping sound. I examined myself, making sure all of my digits were still there.

“What’s the matter, Ricky?” Libby asked, her legs still spread. She adjusted herself on the couch so her vagina was angled higher and better on display.

“Libby, you need to get to a doctor,” I said. “There’s something inside of you. A worm…or…or—" my mind was racing as I stared at her, trying to avoid looking at her cunt.

Libby laughed, but something wasn't right. It sounded like she had a mouthful of fabric…or wet leaves. "There's nothing to be scared of," she said. "I told you, the Goddess saved me and I saved her." Libby reached down and plunged two fingers into her pussy.

Normally, this would be fucking hot, but it was not. She was not really touching herself in a sexual way, but moving her fingers like she was petting something.

"She needed me and I needed her. Now, we both need you." Libby pulled her fingers from her wet vagina and grabbed her lips from either side.

I could only stare at her open pinkness. Something thick and green slithered through her. I gasped, silently stunned. The dark green against the pinkness of her vagina was a harsh contrast. It moved again, working its way through her guts.

Libby rubbed her stomach, smiling. "The Goddess is pleased," she said. "All of your seed has given her strength and renewed her life." She stared away, as if listening again. "But she still needs us, Ricky." A bulge moved in her flat stomach, like a whale about to break the surface.

I'd seen more than enough. "Libby, get dressed. We need to get you to a doctor. You have a parasite or some fucking thing inside of you." I was not dressed for public, but at least my erection was starting to fade. Nothing like seeing a vine or fucking snake in your wife's cunt to kill the mood.

"Come on, Libs," I said, walking to the front door, grabbing my keys along the way.

Libby still hadn't moved, still on the couch spread eagle.

"Fine, I'm going then." I reached up and grabbed the doorknob, not really planning on going anywhere, but maybe I could bluff her into getting dressed at least.

"No," Libby said, her voice even more distorted.

I heard a squelching sound, like pulling a boot from the mud, and turned to look.

A vine, a thin vine no wider than my finger, shot from my wife's vagina. I could see it coming at me, but damn that thing was fast. I put my hand up, the one with the keys, to defend myself.

A burning like nothing I'd ever felt before lit-up my hand. The keys fell to the floor as the vine burrowed through my flesh and bone.

"What the fuck!" I screamed, watching the vine blast through the back of my hand.

Broken shards of bone, and a healthy stream of blood, surrounded the wound. The vine didn't stop. It wound around my fingers.

"You have upset the Goddess," Libby said.

More vines, most of which were much thicker, worked their way out of her pussy. Her lips tore as she gave an unholy birth on the couch, but she didn't even flinch.

I started pulling at the vine around my fingers with my free hand. They felt like braided steel, but still I pulled, trying to unwind them. "Fuck!" I yelled, trying to find purchase on the green demons.

Without warning, the vine jerked, snapping my fingers. At first, the pain didn't come. I just stared like a moron as my four fingers (my thumb was saved from the finger massacre) touched the back of my hand. Then the pain came.

"Holy fuck!" I screamed. I didn't even notice the other vines around my legs. White bone peeked out where my knuckles exploded from the skin. There wasn't as much blood, but at that point, I didn't fucking care; I just needed to get out, just to open the door and scream.

Using my free hand, I started feeling for the doorknob. The realization I had vines around my ankles hit me just before they pulled my feet from under me. I stared at the ceiling for a split second before the back of my head hit the floor. I was never an athlete, but my buddies from school always talked about 'seeing stars' when getting a good hit. It was a weird thing to realize at that moment, but my world lit up like a host of galaxies were living in my eyes. Blood was filling my mouth and I realized I had bit my tongue. It wasn't terrible, I'd done worse eating pizza, but fuck did it hurt.

"The Goddess needs you," Libby said, her voice completely foreign to me. "She needs you."

More and more vines wrapped around me, pulling me away from the door. I swung my unbroken hand, hoping to get purchase on something, anything, to keep me away from my wife.

Another vine slithered over my free arm. Clearly it didn't want me reaching for anything. The tip, which looked dull, plunged into my forearm.

"Fuck your whore mother!" I screamed as the vine split my arm into two. Both bones (their names escape me at the moment) separated like a flat chicken wing. My hand fared no better. When the little bones of my wrist exploded in white shrapnel, my hand ripped like wet canvass. The flesh had nothing on the power of the vines, and my thumb and pointer went one way, and the rest another.

As concerned about my arms as I was, I was more worried about the vines snaking around my lower body. I felt a bunch of them make their way under my shirt. I kicked my legs, but they were loosely held by another bundle of green.

"No, Libby, please fucking stop!" I yelled to her, but she wasn't even paying attention.

Again, Libby stared into the ether, while those things crawled from her box.

If I survived this fucking mess, I would never look at pussy the same way again.

Something pressed against my bellybutton.

"Oh, fuck!"

The pressure was other-worldly, as it pushed, burrowing through the lint and into the creases of my flesh.

"Fuck!"

Then, I felt it inside of me, an insidious creature burrowing into my guts. It could've been the pain, but I could swear I felt it spread, like little fingers.

More vines probed my chest. The violence of my hands and arms seemed like a thing of the past. The vines were on a mission, and I didn't like it. The one over my heart lingered, tickling my nipple. It would've been funny if my arms weren't destroyed and I didn't have a vine in my stomach. Slowly, it began to work into the flesh.

"Motherless fuck!" I felt the tiny tendrils working between my ribs, surrounding my racing heart. They must've squeezed, because a pressure like nothing I'd ever felt threatened to blow my brain apart.

Then, I saw it. The thickest, fattest, and most disturbing vine yet was making its way towards me. The others ended in a nice taper, like a vine should. Not that big motherfucker, it was the size of my leg and ended in an oozing hole.

The smaller vines around my legs began to pull, not at my flesh, but at my pants.

My cock was exposed, and I saw what the large vine was looking for. "No, please, God no. Anything but that!" I was still trying to kick, but the pain, and vines made that an impossibility.

The oozing vine was at my foot, then ankle, slowly working its way to my junk.

I whispered a little prayer, hoping it would be quick and I'd die soon.

A drip of slime landed on my dick and something happened, something I never would've expected in a million years.

I got hard. Not just erect, but full-blown, painfully hard.

"What the fu—" I started, and then the vine wrapped around my entire cock.

It was like nothing I'd ever felt before in my life. A pleasure like the sun was exploding. A pleasure to almost override the pain and torment of my body. I couldn't help it. I came, and came a lot. My cock pumped jizz, what felt like gallons, into the slimy hole of the vine. I thought I'd never stop cumming, until finally, it ebbed away. The vine, however, stayed attached.

"Perfect," Libby grumbled. "The Goddess is happy with you. You will make a good partner and host." Libby smiled, and for just a flash, I could see a vine in her mouth.

I'm sure you thought the story was over, but it's not, sorry. I have just a little more to tell.

I've lost track of time since the Goddess decided to use my body as a human placenta.

Libby pushed something out of her a couple of days ago, or maybe weeks, I'm not sure. It came out looking like a green blob, like a clump of moss and earth. Nothing really too crazy, oh besides the vines attached to it that were feeding off my body.

But I can't complain, not yet. Libby feeds me, and feeds me a lot. Mostly take-out which is left at the door, but I'm okay with it. The cock-vine will fuck me or suck me, whatever it's doing, a few times a day. That's the only bright light in this whole fucking debacle.

I do sleep, but it feels induced, like the clump of green shit is doing it. I still refuse to refer to it as the *Goddess*, even though Libby does. Crazy bitch.

When I woke up the other day, the clump had grown quite a bit. I could see the roundness of what looked like a head with two eyes. The eyes creep me out, always staring at me, except when they blink. That's fucking weird too, because they don't blink horizontal like a human, but vertical. Whatever.

No, that's not my real issue. My real issue was this morning when I woke up.

The clump was bigger again, with four nubs of arms poking out of a torso area. They didn't have fingers or hands, just little stumps.

They didn't bother me, but the clump grew something else that did.

Sitting under the eyes, which are the size of saucers now, is a dripping mouth full of fanged teeth.

The clump is staring at me, and I'm staring at the teeth. It blinks that weird blink, and smiles.

... OF DOUGH AND CINNAMON

Friedman's Bakery smelled like heaven on earth. Fresh bread, pastries, and rugelach—Sarah's specialty—steamed in their respective bins. It was still early, just after 4 a.m., but the store would be opening soon, letting the bustling Brooklyn crowds in for their breakfast.

Dov Friedman carried a tray of fresh bagels in his arms. The display case was closed on his side, and he couldn't seem to nudge it open with his knee.

"Sarah," Dov said, calling for his daughter.

Sarah came out from the small kitchen. Her curly, black hair was tied back in a red bandana, and there was a dusting of flour on her apron.

Dov nodded towards the closed display door.

Sarah slid in front of her father and opened the door, holding it so he could put the bagels into the basket.

He set the tray on the counter. "Thank you," Dov said, pulling a handkerchief from his back pocket to wipe his head.

Even though it was early in the morning, the temperature was nearing eighty degrees already. The addition of the ovens running at full blast didn't help. When it was 5 a.m., Dov would open the front door and keep it propped, hoping to get a slight cross breeze in his little bakery.

Sarah closed the door on the case. "Anything else? I need to finish the cinnamon rugelach and get them in the oven."

Dov took a seat at the stool behind the counter. It was a family heirloom, a piece of furniture used by his father and grandfather when they'd first opened the bakery. Long dead, the patriarchs of the Friedman family created a well-known, and respected, establishment. Dov did everything he could to keep it open.

"No, I have more trays of bagels, but I'll wait for a few minutes before finishing them up." He checked his watch. "I'll finish them soon so they're hot when the doors open."

"Okay," Sarah said, walking back into the kitchen.

Dov watched her go, the door swinging shut behind her. Every day, she got a little older. She turned twenty-one the week before, and every day she looked more and more like her mother. Dov took a deep breath, willing the tears away which seemed to arrive every time he thought of his late wife.

Six years prior, Chana, his wife of thirty-two years, was diagnosed with breast cancer. She was a strong woman, salt of the earth, but the vile disease gave her no quarter. Within eight months of diagnosis, Chana was dead. It rained on the day of her funeral. Even the skies wept when she passed from the realm of the living and into the arms of her God.

Dov crumbled like old bread. His world had been crippled and if it weren't for Sarah, he would have withered away to nothing.

Sarah.

She was the reason he was still breathing. She was the reason Friedman's was still open and producing some of the best baked goods in all of the city. Sarah was the glue holding him together, and she was the last thing he had left in the world. His parents were both many years dead, and his only brother was killed in a car accident as a teenager. It was only Dov, Sarah, and the bakery.

Dov looked at the city streets, which were starting to glow with the rising of the early morning sun. He checked his watch again, realizing nearly a half-hour had passed since he sat down. His reverie had robbed him of precious time, but filled his mind with happier ones, followed by sad ones. He stood, listening to the many creaks and pops his body made. One hand went to his aching back, and the other to the counter, providing him with balance. He was only fifty-six, but felt like a man in his eighties.

Sarah came out with a tray of assorted pastries, fresh and steaming. She was just in time, because the clock above the door was minutes away from 5 a.m. "I took care of the last trays of bagels, Dad," she said, loading the pastries into the case.

Dov watched, admiring her.

She finished and turned, shocked to find her father standing inches away.

"You know, Sarah, without you I don't know what I would've done." He rubbed her arms. The tears he'd chased away prior returned, a whirlwind of emotion settling on him.

Sarah could see the mist forming in her father's tired eyes. She held the tray in one hand and wrapped him in a tight embrace. Every time she hugged him, she was shocked at how thin he'd become. He felt more and more brittle every day, a shadow of the strong, stout man he once was.

Dov held his daughter, breathing the scent of her. It was all her, but in the recess of his brain, he could smell the ghost of Chana.

Tapping on the front window broke their teary-eyed hug.

Dov turned and looked at the door, noticing the clock above showed it was 5:05.

"Damn," he said, walking around the counter to unlock the door. Pulling it open, he saw his first customer of the day.

"Oy, I thought you forgot about me," Ezra Rywski said as he walked into the bakery, his cane supporting him.

Dov smiled at his old friend and long-time customer. "Forget about you? My best customer and family friend? Never." He patted the old man on the back.

If Dov was brittle, then Ezra was downright frail. He was ninety years old, but still did it all. He lived alone, was widowed for nearly forty years, and never had children. During World War II (he always called it 'the war' as if there were never any other ones), his family had been killed or lost. After, he fled to America. He received a letter from his brother, Josef, but that was it. No follow-up, and no more contact.

Sarah came around the counter wiping her hands on her stained apron. "Mr. Rywski," she said, kissing the old man on his smooth cheek. "How nice to see you."

Ezra smiled. Every day they played this game, and every day he looked forward to it.

"Please, Sarah, I've known you since you were a pink, little thing. Call me Ezra." He told her this every morning, but still, she never listened.

"Sure thing, Mr. Rywski," she smirked, walking behind the counter and plucking a couple of rugelach out. She put them on a plate and brought them out to him.

"Thank you." Ezra pulled out a chair at one of the small tables as Sarah set the plate down.

"Coffee this morning?" Sarah asked. A stray curl of hair had sprung free and sat just above her brown eyes.

Ezra rubbed his stomach. "No, I'll have a very light tea."

Sarah grabbed his drink just as the morning rush arrived.

***

Summertime in New York City saw a massive influx of tourists, but that was mainly reserved for Manhattan. The small corner of Brooklyn where Friedman's was wasn't much of a tourist locale. It was old school, full of families who fled the Nazis or left the old countries before

Adolf's reign of terror. Either way, the people of the neighborhood were always on the quest for something better to help the next generation. Some left for good, but most would come back.

A trio of those who made their way home walked through the door of the bakery as Sarah was wiping down the coffee station. It was almost noon: closing time.

"Sarah Friedman," a voice said from behind.

Sarah noticed customers enter, but paid them no mind, figuring they would go to the counter and wait. She stopped cleaning and turned.

Ari Kohn, Lieb Blau, and David Taub stood behind her. It was Ari who spoke, but his eyes were doing the talking then. He looked Sarah up and down, lingering on her breasts, which were tight against her apron.

Reflexively, she crossed her arms and looked away. "Oh, hi Ari," she said, not wanting to look at the young man.

"What are we, chopped liver?" David said in a joking, yet serious, tone. He smacked Lieb, getting his attention.

"Yeah, we just wanted to drop in and grab a few loaves if you have any left," Ari said, looking towards the display cases. "My mother is having a little get-together, you know, to welcome us all home from college."

Sarah smiled the most forced smile of her life. The bakery was her legacy, but she always yearned for more. College, maybe, but to leave her small section of the city, to see the world, to learn, to love, to experience the life that was being wasted on the miscreants in front of her.

"Sure, we have a few left." She turned and began walking towards the counter.

A hand grabbed her ass, squeezing it.

"Hey!" she said, turning around.

It was David who was pulling his hand back, a wry grin on his face.

"Don't touch me."

David put his hands up in mock surrender. "Sorry, you had something on your pants. I was just trying to help." His lie was so thinly veiled, a blind man could see through it, but they were there to buy and their money was green. "Jeez, next time I'll let you walk around with it."

Sarah stilled her temper, taking a deep breath.

"Is there a problem out here?" Dov asked as he walked out of the kitchen. He was drying his hands on a towel, but his eyes were locked on the three young men.

"No, Mr. Friedman. We were just picking up a few loaves of bread for dinner," Ari looked at Sarah, "and catching up with Sarah. That's all." He had the glare of a viper and a tongue of poison.

Dov watched them as Sarah walked back behind the counter. He shuffled up to the display case and grabbed a few loaves of bread. His hands were shaking and Sarah moved close to him.

"It's okay," she said, touching his back. "I'm fine."

Dov licked his lips, took a deep breath, and bagged the bread. "That'll be $6, boys." Dov set the bag on the counter and rang them up.

"Six bucks for day-old bread?" Ari complained, but still pulled out his wallet. "I thought day old was half price?"

He was right, of course, but their attitude and downright disrespect for Sarah warranted a full-price transaction.

"Sorry boys, bills to pay," Dov said, laughing inside.

These kids had more money in their trust funds than three generations of his family combined. They were the last ones who should be complaining about money.

Dov took the money and dropped it into the register.

Ari grabbed the bag and looked at Sarah. "There's a party tonight," he smiled, showing off his expensive dental work. "It's in the backroom over at Rush, but I can put you on the list if you're interested."

Sarah looked at him and did little to hide her disdain and disgust. "No thanks, I already have plans," she said, taking out her towel and wiping down the already clean doors of the display case. That was it, conversation over.

Ari sneered. "Fine. We'll see you around." He turned and walked out the door, David and Lieb in tow.

***

Within an hour, the bakery was clean and the next day's prep work was finished. Sarah tied the laundry bag tight and left it by the back door for the late-night linen service.

"So, what are your plans tonight?" Dov asked, flipping off the lights in the kitchen as they walked out.

Sarah shouldered her purse, checking her cell phone.

"Well, Denise and Carol wanted to go to the village to see a comedy show. I was thinking about catching the bus and heading there."

Sarah watched her father deflate. It was her curse: stay home and be miserable, watching game shows with her father until he fell asleep in front of the TV, or upset him by leaving for the night. She wasn't his wife, she was his twenty-one-year-old daughter with a life of her own.

Dov forced a smile. "That sounds like a great time," he said, pulling his wallet out.

"Dad, no." Sarah stopped and reached for her father's hand, but he already had a stack of bills clenched in his fist.

"Take it," he said, holding out the money. "Take it and have fun." He pushed the money into her hands. "Just not too much fun, I need you baking bright and early." He smiled as she took the cash from him.

Sarah held it in a messy wad as she leaned in and kissed her father on the cheek. "Thank you. I won't be late." She smiled. "Well, I'll be at work. That's a fact." She laughed.

Dov joined and, for a second, all was right with the world.

By the next morning, Dov's world would be destroyed.

***

The city streets were never truly dark. Even though it was 10 p.m., the streetlights bathed the sidewalks in yellow, and Sarah stayed away from the alleys as she walked.

Her bus, the one which had a stop only a block from her building, broke down. The replacement was coming from Mid-Town, and she didn't want to wait the hour for it to arrive. Besides, she was only ten blocks from home. It was better to walk than to wait.

The night was warm and Sarah's skin was sticky with sweat. The comedy club was small, an intimate and cozy setting, but also a damn furnace. The ancient air conditioner did next to nothing, and she doubted the owners even had it on.

Cars whizzed by and she thought about hailing a taxi, but her fiscally-responsible self thought better, and she kept walking. She was almost always aware of her surroundings, but somehow, she didn't notice the Mercedes SUV slowing down.

***

Ari was behind the wheel of his father's Mercedes Benz GLS450. He had a bottle of vodka in one hand, and the other on the wheel. "Here, hold this," he said, passing the bottle to David, who was in the front seat.

David grabbed it just before it fell into his lap.

"Pass that up," Ari said to Lieb, who was smoking a joint in the backseat.

Lieb pinched the joint and handed it up to Ari, careful not to burn him, or even worse, the seats.

Ari smoked the potent weed, taking it deep into his lungs. His head swam as a cloud of smoke rose before his eyes. He coughed, hit it again, and passed it back to Lieb. "Gimmee the bottle," Ari demanded, looking over at David. "Hey," he swatted his friend on the arm, "gimmee that shit."

David wasn't paying attention. His drug-addled brain was focused on something outside. Not something, but some*one*. "There's the fucking bitch," he slurred.

They intended to pre-game before going to Rush, but whatever pills Lieb scored were a bit stronger than the Xanax they were used to.

"Huh?" Ari asked, slowing the car down so he could see what his friend was looking at.

"Fucking Sarah," David said, as if in disbelief.

Ari saw her walking and slowed down. "Let's see if she needs a ride," he grinned, pulling the car to the curb.

"Oh, I'll give that stuck-up cunt a ride, alright," Lieb chimed in from the backseat.

"Hey Sarah," David said, rolling down the tinted window.

She looked up, recognized the young men in the car, and began walking even faster.

Ari kept up with her alongside the road.

"Do you want a ride?" David asked, gesturing to the inside of the car. "There's plenty of room."

Lieb put the back window down."Yeah, you can sit back here with me." He sneered, but tried to sound charming.

"No thanks, but I appreciate it." She picked up her pace to just under a light jog.

"Oh, come on, Sarah," Ari yelled. "Just get in the car." He felt the rim of the wheel grind the curb.

Sarah didn't respond, just kept walking.

"Sarah!" Ari screamed, making her jump. "Get in the fucking car!"

She broke into a full sprint, running down the street.

The few people on the block didn't even look; worse things were happening in the city that doesn't sleep.

Her flats came off and the rough sidewalk chewed up the soles of her feet. She left bloody footprints as she ran. Shards of glass stabbed her, and cigarette butts clung to the blood.

"Help!" she screamed, running from the pursuing SUV.

The one thing about New Yorkers: they don't give a fuck unless it's happening to them.

Sarah reached an intersection, the SUV bearing down on her. If she didn't stop, she'd be run over. She stopped, her feet sliding in her slick blood.

"Fucking grab her!" Ari yelled. "Fucking cunt made me curb my rims."

Lieb threw open the back door and grabbed her.

Sarah punched and kicked, but she was tired from running.

Lieb began swinging, his fist hitting her stomach and taking the fight out of her. "Go, go, go!" he said once he got her in the vehicle.

Ari peeled out, sending the big SUV into the night. He flew down a few dark streets, a rarity in the city. He knew exactly where he was going.

***

The old school stood dark, like an ancient monolith. It was closed after 9/11 and hadn't been reopened.

Ari drove around back and killed the lights. "Okay, Sarah, let's see what you're made of." He climbed over the seat, unbuckling his pants as he did.

Sarah screamed again and kicked out at him.

"Fuck! Lieb, hold her down would you?"

Lieb hit her again as Ari pulled her dress up.

"Ah, so that's what you're working with." He ripped her underwear off, staring at a thatch of black pubic hair leading to a bald slit. "Boys, this is going to be a hell of a night," he laughed.

Sarah screamed.

***

Sarah was battered, broken, and bloody, but she was alive. She lay in a stupor on the plush backseat of the Mercedes. Her throat was raw from screaming and she felt like she inhaled glass.

"What the fuck are we going to do?" David asked, a fresh bottle of booze hovered under his lips. He took a sip, grimaced, and handed it to Lieb.

"Get rid of her," Ari said, his dark eyes staring at nothing.

"What the fuck do you mean *get rid of her*?" Lieb asked, drinking from the bottle. He had an unlit joint behind his ear.

"Kill her, dump her, go to Rush like nothing fucking happened, that's what I mean." Ari ripped the bottle from Lieb's mouth and a stream of alcohol landed on his shirt.

"Hey, what the fuck?" Lieb wiped at the wetness, but it was in vain.

"What else are we going to do? Let her go? We'll go to fucking prison." Ari stated, as if it were a matter of fact. "Even my dad couldn't get us out of that, not with her testimony and —" he paused, a realization hitting him. "Fuck! We didn't use rubbers. Our fucking jizz is in her."

He rubbed his head in frustration, spitting in disgust. How could he have been so stupid? The fucking drugs and booze, that's how. In college, if he was a little *forceful,* he always wore a rubber. This was different, he was careless.

"Fuck, man," Lieb said. The realization of what they'd done set in. He looked at David. "We have no choice. She needs to go."

David stared into space and nodded. "I agree, but what are we going to say?"

Ari took a deep breath, willing his brain to clear. "Fire. We have to torch her. Kill her and set her ass on fire." It could work, and hopefully destroy the evidence. Ari licked his lips. "I'll fucking do it. I'll kill her."

The other two stared at him, a silent weight of relief was lifted from them.

"You sure?" David asked, hoping his friend didn't go back on his word. Even drunk and high, he didn't think he could kill her.

Ari nodded. "Yeah. Get her out of the car."

The other two stood frozen.

"Now!" he yelled, his voice echoing off the buildings.

Lieb and David moved, opening the back doors of the car.

"Hey, Ari, we have a problem here," David called to his friend.

"What?" Ari asked, walking over.

The overhead lights showed a mess. Sarah lay in a stupor, coagulated blood and semen seeped into the seats and floor mats.

"There's no way we'll be able to clean that, and if the cops come looking, we're fucked," David said, as if they didn't know that.

"My dad loves this car, but I'm not going to fucking prison," Ari said as he walked to the back of the car.

He opened the back liftgate, and then opened a box in the back. Bottles of liquor stood in there, each separated by pieces of cardboard. He searched through them and pulled two out. They were special edition, and 80% alcohol. He was saving them for the club, hoping to get a few girls beyond their limit, but they'd have to be used for a different girl.

"Here," he said, handing a bottle to David. "Dump this on the front seats." He shut the hatch. "I'll take the back."

David dumped the bottle on the seats, not wanting to look at Sarah in the back.

"Ari," Sarah gasped. Her face was battered and bloody. Her left eye was swollen shut and her teeth were shattered. "Please," she reached with broken fingers, begging him to stop.

Ari pulled the cork from the bottle and dumped it on Sarah.

She screamed. The potent alcohol burned her open wounds. Writhing in pain, she tried squirming towards the exit.

Ari watched her crawl. *Pathetic,* he thought. He grabbed the lighter from his pocket, heart racing. He touched it to Sarah's bloody foot. There was no turning back. Ari spun the wheel of the lighter. Flame, the bluest flame he'd ever seen, engulfed Sarah. He slammed the door, sealing her in.

She screamed, but the roar of the fire drowned out her cry.

Ari, Lieb, and David stepped back and watched black smoke pour from the seams in the car. A black hand, charred and bloody pressed against the glass, then was gone. The fire roiled, engulfing the luxury car and the girl inside of it.

Ari looked at David and punched him in the face.

"Ow, what the fuck?" David asked, holding his swelling eye.

"Hit me," Ari said, standing in front of the inferno. He slapped himself in the face.

"What?" David asked, confused. His mind was racing and a dull ache from the punch had him seeing double.

"Those fucking mutts carjacked us, right?" Ari said, stepping closer to David. "They sucker punched you, and when we got out, they attacked us," he pointed to his chest and Lieb's. "Beat us up and stole the car."

David and Lieb were starting to catch on.

Before he could react, Ari punched Lieb in the face, breaking his nose.

"You motherfucker!" Lieb yelled, cradling his nose, which was gushing blood. He lowered his head and tackled his friend.

Ari's head hit the pavement, splitting his scalp.

Lieb punched him a few times, cutting his lip.

"Okay, okay, fuck," Ari said, raising his hands in defense.

Lieb helped him up with a bloody hand.

They watched the car smolder, flames still alive.

"Come on, let's get the fuck out of here and call the cops."

Dov woke to loud banging on his apartment door. His alarm clock, which sat next to a picture of him, Chana, and Sarah, said it was only 2:50 a.m. He was supposed to be up in 10 minutes and couldn't believe he was losing sleep.

The banging rattled the doorframe, and it finally registered in his sleep-deprived brain. It had to be Sarah. She must've forgotten her keys and was locked out.

"I'm coming," he said, putting slippers on. "Sarah, do you know what time it is?" He unlocked the door and opened it. "We need to leave in—"

Two NYPD detectives stood solemnly with Rabbi Kirsh behind them.

"Dov, we need to talk about Sarah," Rabbi Kirsh said.

Dov's head began to spin. It was all a blur. The visions of Chana in bed, the doctor telling him she was gone. It was that again, but worse. Blackness closed in around him, sucking him down, pulling him to the ground. He couldn't fight it, he wanted the earth to open and swallow him.

The detectives caught Dov before he hit the ground.

***

"I'm sorry, Mr. Friedman. There's no evidence those boys had anything to do with the murder of your daughter," Detective Barca said, dismissing the grieving father for the third time that week. "Now, if we get any leads on the individuals who stole the car, we'll be sure to reach out to you, but for now, that's all we have."

Dov shook, the phone vibrating against his ear.

"Again, I'm sorry for your loss and I'll be in touch."

The line went dead.

Dov held the receiver against his ear, waiting for the shrill wail of the 'off the hook' sound. He dropped the phone into the cradle and put his face in his hands. Tears, hot and full of rage, grief, and anguish, poured from his eyes. He screamed, willing Sarah back to life, praying for her salvation and promising his eternal soul for just another hug from her, another smile from her, anything. He sat in his chair, wiping the snot across his stubbly cheeks, not caring about it.

There was a knock at the door. It didn't sound like a fist, but a solid object.

"Dov, open the door," a voice said from the hallway.

He turned, willing his visitor away.

The knock sounded again, followed by a hacking cough.

"It's Ezra, Ezra Rywski, your favorite customer." There was a pause, a cough, and another knock.

Dov rose. His clothes felt grimy and stuck to his body. He unlocked the door and opened it to Ezra, who stood there with his cane in one hand and a bottle of bourbon in the other.

"Thanks." Ezra pushed into the apartment. He looked around and moved towards the couch. He collapsed and set the bottle down. "Get some cups."

Dov was in a fog. Moments earlier, he was thinking about death, but then, he was about to have a drink with an old customer. As if on auto-pilot, he went into the kitchen and grabbed two glasses.

"Ah, thanks," Ezra said, taking the cups and setting them down. He opened the bottle and poured a generous amount into each one. He raised his glass in a silent toast, waiting for Dov to do the same.

Dov raised his cup as well.

"HaShem yikom dama," Ezra said, throwing back his drink in one gulp.

Dov put his head back and swallowed the hard liquor. He winced and put the cup down, motioning Ezra to fill it again. Dov put back another one, the alcohol hitting his depleted bloodstream.

Ezra put his cup down and stared at Dov. "Have I ever told you about the pure evil of man?" he asked, rolling up his sleeve to show a faded tattoo of numbers inked on his forearm. "Bah, I don't have to tell you." Ezra took another small drink and pushed the bottle away. What he was about to tell his friend needed a little liquid courage, but too much and he'd be sleeping.

"I know about evil, Ezra. Oh, I fucking know."

"When they, the Nazis, came for us, I was terrified. I was only a boy, but I wanted to fight back, wanted to rally the men and kill them. Fight those fuckers off, kill them all. We had a grand rabbi, Lipshitz, who told the men to fight, repel the invaders, to protect our way of life, our women and children, our homes." He was getting drunk, but didn't care.

Dov poured more in both cups.

The men drank, their grimaces becoming less.

"The rabbi was old, as old as I am now, but he had the heart of a warrior. But, his body was far from a fighter. He needed a champion, but our men were scared. The Nazis had guns, tanks, and trained soldiers. What could a few scared Jews do against that? Well, Rabbi Lipshitz had a way. A dreadful, cursed way, but a way. The Nazis took up residence in the village, occupying a home. It wasn't many of them, but a small unit of men. In the night, they were slaughtered, ripped apart in a brutal, violent way that was obscene to God and man, torn limb from limb. It was blamed on rebels, and many men paid for the attack with their lives, not willing to give up any names. They would've if they knew who attacked the unit, but they didn't." He was glassy-eyed and slurring worse. "I know who it was," Ezra spat.

Dov was listening intently. For a moment his woes were almost forgotten. "Who was it? The rabbi?"

Ezra nodded. "Yes and no. It was a golem, a monster of earth and clay, summoned by the rabbi."

"A golem? Like from the Torah?"

Ezra nodded again. "Exactly, but this beast was different. The Torah tells us the golem is uncontrollable, given a task and set to it. They have no thought, just perform their tasks and go back to the earth. The rabbi found a different way, a way to make the monster into his champion, but at a cost." He took another sip of booze. "The rabbi was found dead the next morning. His heart stopped and a pile of dirt was at his front door. He was part of the golem, and the golem was part of him, and together, they died."

"Why are you telling me this?" Dov asked. He was seeing double, the alcohol dulling his mind.

Ezra had a drunken glint in his eyes. "Because, we're going to fucking get them," he filled the glasses again. "HaShem yikom dama," he said. "May HaShem avenge her blood."

***

It had been almost two weeks since the murder of Sarah, and finally, the cops left David alone.

The first couple of days had been touch and go, with the questions coming rapid-fire, but they all stuck to the story of the carjacking. The corroboration, and the fact Ari's father was a powerful, well-known attorney, helped, which was good; they were home on break and didn't want anything hampering their good time.

Speaking of good times, David was on a mission: buy drugs for the party that night. The last time they tried to have fun, they encountered Sarah, and the night went to shit. At least they got to fuck, but ended up in a tricky situation for a while.

David parked his car in a less-than-desirable part of Brooklyn. His dealer, Grimy, ran the block. Anyone fucking with a customer of his would pay dearly. That was the way to do business.

Grimy was just that, grimy, but David had been buying drugs from him since middle school. His prices were better than that of the Jewish kids in his community who would always jack them up. David went to the source.

The streets were busy, and David ended up having to park on the opposite side of Grimy's building. He looked at his BMW, hoping it would be okay. His wellbeing was accounted for, but his car was another story. He was able to park in a space behind a closed Chinese restaurant, which was behind Grimy's building. David eyed up the dark alley, which would take him straight to the front of the building. He hated alleys, and avoided them at all cost, but time was of the essence. He spent too long circling the block looking for parking and was going to be late. Ari was already in a bad mood and David didn't want to feel his wrath for some stupid shit.

He took out his cell phone and turned on the flashlight feature. The small LED gave him a little light, but not nearly enough to dispel all the shadows. He entered the alley, watching his footing around piles of garbage. A smell hit him—fresh bread and cinnamon. He was pleasantly surprised; most alleys smelled like human waste and garbage.

"Huh, must be a bakery on the other side," he said aloud, thinking of when a bakery had opened in the area.

He saw a massive pile of garbage ahead, and moved as close to the wall as possible without touching it. As David closed in, he realized the smell of baked goods was coming from the garbage pile. He shined his light at the trash.

The garbage pile, which looked like a blob of semi-baked dough, began to move.

David stood frozen with fear. Only his hand moved, using the light to follow the monster's ascent, which never seemed to stop, until in front of him, standing eight feet tall, was a demon, a monster, a golem.

It looked soft and squishy, like it was proofed dough because that's what it was. Its shape was humanoid, but it was devoid of any human features, save for its eyes. Where a human's eyes should be sat two perfect swirls of cinnamon rugelach.

David watched, terrified, only a squeak coming from his throat as the creature began to reach towards its stomach.

Knives stuck out of the golem's belly, knives of every shape and form. There was even a rolling pin. The golem grabbed a butcher knife, old and well used, and slid it from its body.

Finding his senses, David turned to run, but the golem was too fast. A doughy paw wrapped around his neck, stopping him and pulling him close to the baked beast.

The golem raised the knife, relishing the fear in the eyes of the young man, and plunged the blade in the crook of David's neck, right where his collar bone was.

The hardened steel made short work of flesh and bone. Blood flew and David's world began to fade to black, but the golem kept stabbing. Each pull of the knife was wetter, throwing more gore onto its tan flesh.

David fell dead, his lifeblood flowing onto the dirty alley floor. He was nearly decapitated, with severed tendons and blood vessels exposed.

The golem plunged the knife back into its belly; its work was far from over.

***

"This motherfucker is late again," Ari said, looking at his phone for the tenth time in two minutes. "He probably tested the shit and passed out." He put his phone back in his pocket and walked over to his dresser.

"Next time," Lieb, who was sitting at Ari's computer desk playing an online game, said, "I'll get the drugs. I like them as much as the next guy, but I know better."

"Yeah, sure." Ari ignored him, rifling through his sock drawer until he found a small box. "I hope this is still full." He pulled the box out and set it on the dresser.

Luckily for him, it was full. Pills, ranging in color, size, and make-up, looked back at him. There was a small bag of weed, but it was dry. They'd still smoke it, but it probably wasn't the best.

"Perfect," Ari said, filling his pockets with the narcotics. He took his phone out and checked it again, but not thinking about his friend. "The car should be here any minute. Let's go wait."

Lieb's character in the game died in a blast of gunfire and a red screen. "Sounds good." He shut down the computer and followed his friend out to the street.

It wasn't unlike David to flake on them. In college, if he hooked up with a girl, he'd go missing for a day or two, only to resurface as if nothing had happened.

They didn't have to wait long before their ride pulled up. A brand new Cadillac, sleek and black, stopped in front of the building. It had a rental car barcode on the window, but Ari and Lieb didn't seem to care.

"That was fast," Ari said, sliding into the backseat.

"Yeah, we just walked out." Lieb followed his friend in through the same door, making him slide over.

"I'm always on time," the old man behind the wheel said.

Ari and Lieb looked at each other when they heard the old man talk. He sounded ancient and it was dark.

"Hey, grandfather, are you okay to drive in the dark?" Ari asked, partially joking and partially serious.

The old man laughed. "Young man, I'm perfectly fine and my vision is sharp. Now, please buckle up. My name is Ezra, and I'll get you right where you need to be."

Ezra pulled away from the curb and began driving. He had a mission, a destination, and he was getting there one way or another. He turned, the wrong way of where the boys wanted to go, but neither said anything.

Another wrong turn and finally one spoke up. "Do you know a shortcut or something?"

"Yeah, I've been in this city longer than most of the buildings. You'll be fine."

A couple more turns and another complaint. "I think you're lost, gramps. Pull over and I'll drive," Ari said from the backseat.

Ezra ignored him; they were almost there. He pressed the accelerator, throwing them into the seats.

"Hey, what the fuck are you doing? Are you trying to fucking kill us?" Lieb yelled, thankful he listened and buckled his seatbelt.

Ezra drove, seeing his destination in the distance: the old school.

"What the fuck!" yelled Ari, realizing where they were.

Ezra pulled in, stopped the car, and turned off the lights.

A massive man stood waiting in the distance.

The night smelled of dough and cinnamon as Ezra jumped out of the car. He locked the doors on his way out.

Ari pulled at the door handle, realizing the child locks were engaged.

Lieb figured it out too, and climbed over the seats to the front doors. He flung open the passenger side door and started to run.

In the moonlight, Ari watched the giant move.

It didn't look human. Besides the fact it was eight feet tall, it looked like a man in a wrinkled fat suit. The monstrosity pulled something from its stomach; it was a cleaver. It wound up like a baseball player, and hurled the blade.

Silvery light glinted off the sides as it flew true, landing in Lieb's lower back.

"Ah, fuck!" Lieb screamed, falling face first in the parking lot.

The golem lurched over to the injured boy. The beast grabbed and twisted the knife handle, cracking the pelvic bone in which it was embedded.

Ari watched in fear as the monster raised the blade and began hacking away at his friend.

Blood, bone, and grey matter all flew into the night air. Lieb was dead, but the monster hacked and hacked, until the cleaver was stuck in the asphalt.

Ari needed to make a break for it, and seized his opportunity. He scrambled out of the car, forgetting about Ezra.

The old man had fought evil, knew evil, and wanted to kill evil. With every last bit of strength he could muster, he swung his cane into the back of Ari's skull.

Ari thought he'd been shot, and fell face first, just catching himself from breaking his nose. The smell of bread was almost nauseating as he rolled over and looked at the golem above him.

The monster grabbed him with an unnaturally strong hand and dragged him to the trunk, which Ezra popped open.

Ari saw what was in the car and pissed his pants.

A gas can, full and sloshing, sat waiting.

"No, please God, no," Ari begged, punching into the soft dough of the golem with the cinnamon rugelach eyes.

The golem grabbed the can and pushed Ari to the ground.

Ari fought and kicked, but another arm of dough formed from the golem's body. Two fat hands of dough grabbed his upper and lower jaws, and pried his mouth open. He tried to fight it, but his jaw unhinged, the bone resting on his chest.

Using its third arm, the golem jammed the nozzle of the gas can down Ari's throat.

Cold gasoline flooded his mouth, some spraying from his nose as he coughed it up. His jaw sat slack as he choked on the gas. Ari's throat and sinuses burned from the chemical, but he had no idea what burning was.

The golem reached into its doughy body and pulled out a Zippo lighter. Fine fingers made of dough formed, snapping open the lighter with a *ting* sound.

Ari tried to scream, but without his jaw connected, it was a guttural roar of primal fear. His eyes widened as the orange flame licked at the wick in the lighter.

The golem paused, holding the flame in its hand. Slowly, it turned its head, its rugelach eyes looking at the pathetic, scared man on the floor. It threw the lighter at Ari's face.

He tried to scurry away, but as the flame touched his gas-soaked shirt, a snake of fire, red and orange, slithered up his chest, seeking his mouth. The fire moved almost instantly, but to Ari, it was in slow motion. The chemical burning of the gas was replaced with the fires of Hell. His tongue seared, sticking to his teeth. Flames ate his perfect hair, consuming the product he'd used before his night on the town. In moments, he was dead.

The flames continued to feed, casting a shadow of the golem on the side of the school.

Finally, Ari was nothing more than a charred husk of red and black flesh with the occasional white bone peeking out.

***

Dov sat on a chair in the middle of the bakery. He had snapped back, leaving the body of the vengeful golem, after Ari took his last fiery breath.

It was done.

He was done.

Dov held Sarah's bandana to his nose, breathing her in. He closed his eyes, picturing her, seeing her at every stage from her birth, to her first steps, first words, and even her first cinnamon rugelach. He cried...hard. His baby girl, taken from him in the most vicious of ways by a pack of monsters. Well, they got to see a real monster, to feel the fear she felt and the pain she endured.

Tears fell, wetting the fabric, but still, he smelled her—the sweat, her shampoo, and just the slightest hint of cinnamon.

The door to the bakery opened and heavy, yet soft, footsteps sounded on the floor.

Dov didn't look up, just kept his eyes down, smelling her.

The hulking mass moved closer, its shadow engulfing the small man.

Dov prayed, smelling the scent of Sarah…and then…it was gone.

Replaced by the smell of dough and cinnamon.

THE DEAD NEVER DIE

The paper gown irritated Jane Wykowski's nipples. She fidgeted on the cold exam table, pulling the garment away from her chest, hoping the doctor would come back in soon. She looked around the room, trying to ease her troubled mind, but the posters on the walls did little to help. They did the exact opposite.

Living with cancer was one of them. *How much time do I have?* was another. There were a few more, along with some pamphlets, but she didn't pick them up.

So, she stared straight ahead at the heavy, wooden door, hoping the doctor would come in with good news and send her on her way.

Cancer.

It was the ultimate four-letter word. In her twenty-five years as a police officer, with the last fifteen as a detective, not much scared Jane. Even her two ex-husbands, the first of whom beat the shit out of her regularly, didn't scare her. What *did* scare her was fucking cancer.

Jane's retirement party was supposed to be a time of joy, booze, fried food, and war stories. Instead, it resulted in her passing out and making a fool of herself. She wasn't much of a drinker, and when she felt the darkness closing in, she thought maybe someone spiked her drink as a joke. Her face hit a table on the way down, giving her double black eyes and a bloody nose. Some fucking joke.

It hadn't been a prank, and her colleagues, stoic veterans like herself, called 911.

When she came to, Jane was in the back of an ambulance on her way to the hospital. After some testing and questions, the doctors discovered a mass in her brain which crept down into her spinal cord.

The day had finally come. Results day.

Jane touched her face, which was still tender from the party. Only a few days ago, she was on top of the world: retired, great pension, a solid savings account, and ready to see the world. Nothing tied her down. She had no kids, pets, or responsibilities. Nope, retired Detective Wykowski was free from the dregs of civil service.

The handle on the door began to move, and Jane's pulse spiked. Her heart thudded and her breath quivered.

Doctor Shenkman, a short, balding man who resembled Bunsen from *The Muppets*, walked in. His eyes were down, looking at her chart. Gently, he closed the door behind him.

Jane watched as he walked over to the stool and set the folder down on the small countertop.

He sat and finally looked at her.

She wanted to puke and felt like the waiting was the worst form of torture ever. Fuck waterboarding, let someone wait for test results. That'll get them to talk.

Dr. Shenkman took off his glasses and looked at her. "I'm sorry, Ms. Wykowski," he began, looking her in the eyes, "it's cancer."

Jane felt her world crumble. She wanted to cry. She wanted to scream about how fucking unfair it was that she was finally done and ready to really live her life, that forty-eight was too young to be given a death sentence. But no, she didn't do any of that. She plastered on her hardcore detective face, the one she used to interrogate suspects. Jane wanted to ask questions, but didn't, afraid her voice would betray her.

Shenkman went on. "I'm going to have you get dressed and meet me in my office." He put his glasses back on, the nose pieces falling into the indentations. "We'll talk," he paused and formed what he was going to say next, "options and a time frame." He closed her file, stood, and walked out of the room.

The door clicked shut with a finality Jane could feel.

Cancer in my fucking brain, she thought. The tears, the twenty-five years of holding them back at the sight of dead kids and mangled bodies, came pouring out.

***

Jane sat in her car. The crying had stopped, but her eyes were still red. She took her cell phone from her purse and unlocked it.

A generic background greeted her, no pictures of family, kids, pets, or even a friend.

She used her thumb to unlock the screen and scrolled through her social media accounts. Jane had a phone call to make, but it was one she dreaded.

Mack had been her partner for the better part of eight years. They shared everything together—laughs, cries, dinner, injuries, and late nights. And once, just after she made detective, they'd shared a kiss. It was stupid and drunken, but it'd happened. They promised to never speak of it again; neither of them thought Mack's wife, Charlotte, would think highly of it. Since that night in the parking lot, they'd never kissed again. It was one of the best moments of Jane's life. She would never tell Mack that, even on her deathbed, but it was.

Jane opened up her 'frequent contacts' tab. Mack's name was at the top, and below him was the burrito place down the street. Her chewed fingernail hovered above his name. Finally, she pressed it. She put the phone to her ear and listened as it connected.

"Good news, I hope." Mack must've been waiting by his phone, because it only rang once before he answered.

Jane felt the hot sting of tears welling up again and took a quivering breath to keep them back. She and Mack never lied to each other (well, almost never) and tried to not sugarcoat things. Jane wanted to break that rule. She wanted to lie and tell him everything was going to be okay, that the incident was nothing and she was in tip-top shape and ready to see the world. No, she couldn't do that to him, not after all those years of trust.

"Cancer," she croaked, phlegm clogging her throat.

Mack was silent on the other line, letting the word hang in the ether between them.

"Did you hear me?" she asked. "I have cancer." Her throat cleared.

Mack heard her the first time, but was numb. It felt like a dream to him. Too many people were killed in the line of duty, or injured. It wasn't rare to retire, but many people didn't. Not only that, the government was banking on the cops to not live long after their final tour. In most cases, they were right.

"I heard you," Mack could finally say. "Treatable?" he sputtered.

"No. Three to six months, tops," Jane said. It felt odd saying that, as if her putting a timeframe made it a real thing and not the fact a massive tumor was in her brain.

Mack sighed. "Okay." He paused, thinking of how to word what he was going to say next. He didn't want to put any ideas in her head, but he needed to know what frame of mind she was in. "Don't do anything…rash."

Jane actually laughed at that. "Like what? Eat my fucking gun?" If she said the thought hadn't crossed her mind, she'd be lying. Jane would never do it, but it was tempting. Maybe in a few months when she was in pain and her body was a shell. If she had the strength, then maybe she'd blow her brains out. But then and there, no. She was good.

"Just…" Mack was never one for interrogations. "Call me if there's any *unwholesome* thoughts."

This made Jane laugh in earnest. "Yeah, I'll be sure to let you know if I'm on any porn sites later. Those are the only unwholesome thoughts I'll be having." The laugh felt good and Jane didn't know how many more good times she'd have.

***

It had been a week since her diagnosis, and Jane still felt pretty damn good. The occasional headache, but those were defeated with Evan Williams and Advil. Of course, once the news broke in her *former* department, she received flowers, booze, and even a few interesting sex toys. Each delivery and phone call brought a little joy to her, knowing her funeral wouldn't be lonely. The thing inside of her was a ticking time bomb, and she was just waiting for it to blow.

Jane sat on the couch with a steaming burrito on the coffee table. She had plans to visit one of the local museums, but a water main leak caused them to close. She was upset and relieved. Jane wanted to see what she could see, at least in the immediate area, but she was tired.

She reached for her food when her cell phone rang. Side-eyed, she looked at it, figuring it was another co-worker checking in, but when she saw it was Dr. Shenkman, she snatched it up.

"Hello," she said.

"Hello, Ms. Wykowski?"

"Speaking."

"This is Dr. Shenkman." He didn't wait for her to respond. "I'm just checking in to see how you're feeling."

She was fine, but knew she wasn't. Each day brought new little things. Like the day before, she spaced out in the kitchen, forgetting what she was doing. Yes, this wasn't uncommon for people to do, but she stood in one spot for ten minutes without touching a thing.

"All things considered, pretty damn good." Jane adjusted the phone and grabbed her burrito. She bit into it. The hot meat burned her tongue.

"Good, that's good," Shenkman replied. The sound of him writing made its way through the phone lines. "I have an offer for you, but please don't feel obligated to accept."

Jane made a *what the fuck* face and put the burrito down. She quickly chewed and swallowed. "What kind of offer?"

Shenkman wrote a little more. "A clinical trial. A new medication to fight non-surgical cancer, like yours."

Jane's heart began racing. She felt like she was getting the bad news all over again, but this time it could be good.

"Now, this is an…experimental medication, you see," Shenkman reiterated. "Nausea, vomiting, hallucinations. They've all been reported as side-effects in the early stages of testing. Please, if you experience any of these, call me immediately."

Jane didn't give a fuck if the meds gave her six tits and twenty fingers. Another shot at life was worth any risk. "Yeah, sure. Test away, I'm fucking in," she said, the excitement in her voice obvious.

"I don't want to get your hopes up. This is a new medication, which is why the company is doing further testing. You're the perfect candidate."

Jane was hardly listening. Of course, she was the perfect candidate; she had inoperable cancer. That was only part of the reason for her selection. The fact she didn't have a family was another, and much bigger, factor.

"When can we start?" she asked.

"Today at 3 p.m., if you can."

"Well, I'll have to check my busy schedule of eating burritos and binge-watching shows I've seen hundreds of times, but I think I can make it." The smile on her face was almost painful.

"Wonderful. I'll see you then."

Jane hit the end button and tossed her phone next to her. A second chance? Maybe. But first, the burrito.

***

The first week on the medication was rough. Jane slept little, and when she did, it was broken and full of nightmares. Memories from her past, things she'd repressed over the years, found their way back to the forefront of her brain. She relied on laxatives if she even wanted a chance at taking a shit. But, after the first week, things started to level out. Sleep and bowel movements came easily. She started checking things off her bucket list, even though she hoped she had more time with the meds.

Jane was brushing her teeth for the night when her phone rang. She looked and saw Mack's name on the screen. She spit and rinsed, getting most of the toothpaste out.

"Hello," she said.

"Hey, I'm just checking in," Mack replied. "I was seeing if you had any plans in the morning. Maybe we could grab some breakfast and just talk for a bit."

Jane wiped her mouth with the hand towel and walked out to her bed. She fell heavily on it, letting the clean sheets catch her.

"No, I don't have anything planned in the morning and breakfast sounds great."

"Awesome. I'll pick you up at eight."

"It's a date," Jane said, suddenly feeling giddy. She didn't know if it was a side effect of the meds or just the new lease on life, but she felt great.

Mack chuckled. "Sure, it's a date. I'll see you tomorrow."

"Goodnight," she said, but he'd already hung up.

***

Jane slept with a fan on. The sound of white noise and moving air helped her fall asleep and stay asleep. When the power would go out, it was like torture. She'd open a sound file of white noise on her phone, but it wasn't the same as the fan. One of the toughest things about her first marriage (besides the beatings and marital rape) was the fact Shawn hated sleeping with the fan. He couldn't stand it, and after a while, decided it wasn't happening anymore.

Jane's subconscious latched onto the white noise of the fan blades, keeping her in her slumber.

The fan stopped.

Her eyes fluttered, but the first thing that hit her was the smell of bad breath. Whiskey breath.

"Janey," a voice said, inches from her ear.

Jane snapped awake, fear gripping her. A wave of nausea washed over her, making bitter vomit rise to the back of her throat. Only one person called her Janey, and when he did, something bad was in store for her.

Shawn stood over the bed, looking down at her as she scrambled away. He took a swig from the neck of a bottle, a little running down his stubbled chin. He was wearing the same clothes and looked identical to the day she finally left him. He crawled onto the bed, chasing her off of it. "Janey, you've been a bad girl, haven't you?" he sneered. To some people it would constitute a smile, but Shawn didn't smile. "Are you fucking Mack again? Huh, you little fucking whore."

Jane rolled off the bed, her head thudding on the ground. She bit her tongue, but not badly. "What the fuck are you doing here?" she asked, backing away as he began stalking her. "You're dead."

Shortly after their divorce, Shawn drove his car into a tree. He was never a fan of seatbelts, condoms, or speed limits. She had to identify his mangled corpse in the morgue.

Dead, dead, dead. He's not real, Jane. You're hallucinating. You're dreaming. Wake up, you dumb bitch, wake up.

Jane pressed her eyes shut, then snapped them back open. The nightmare remained.

Shawn waved at himself, almost as a presentation. "Does it look like I'm dead?" He slugged back another gulp of brown liquor. "The dead never die, Janey," he sneered, wiping his mouth with the back of his hand.

Jane squared up towards the door.

Shawn went for another drink and Jane ran. He was too fast, almost a blur, as he blocked the door, grabbing her.

"Get the fuck off of me!" she yelled in his face, trying to scratch his eyes.

The bottle of booze was gone as he grabbed both of her wrists. "Now, Janey, that's not nice." He pulled her from the room, nearly dislocating her shoulders. They entered the kitchen, and he turned the lights on. "Do you stroke his cock with these fingers?" he asked, holding her hands up to his face.

For a second, she thought he was going to bite her. She pulled, but his grip was unnatural.

"Well, maybe we can make that a little more difficult." He opened a drawer.

"No, please no!" Jane shrieked, pulling against him. She was helpless as he put her fingers inside.

Shawn pulled the drawer as far back as the runners would allow, then gave her another one of his signature smiles, and slammed it shut. The hard edge fractured bone and split skin.

Jane felt the pain immediately. The hot, instant sharpness of a broken bone coursed through her arm. She pulled her hand from the drawer and de-gloved two of her fingers in her haste. She stared at the flesh, rolled down her fingers like a used condom. Shawn was all but forgotten. Her twisted, bleeding fingers were her new priority.

She knew it would come to this one day. She knew he'd return to kill her like he always promised he would. Her back was to the rest of the kitchen as she gathered her reserve to fight him. She looked for a weapon, but the butcher block was too far away for her to grab a knife and not make it obvious. Oh well, she'd have to fight him and hope to God she got lucky. Turning, she swung her fist as hard as possible and hit…nothing but air.

Her frantic eyes searched for him, darting from one corner to the next, but the kitchen was empty. The slow dripping of her blood was the only sound she heard, besides the thudding of her pulse in her head.

Glass shattered in the living room and she let out a little shriek. It wasn't one of fear, but surprise. Jane grabbed a knife from the butcher block and prepared for war.

"Help, please help," a man yelled from the living room.

Jane froze for a moment. *That's not Shawn's voice*, she thought. She moved slowly, keeping her damaged hand against her chest. It wasn't Shawn's voice, but it was one she'd heard before.

A man was on the living room floor, and in front of him was a girl covered in blood. "Oh, thank God," the man said, looking up from the girl.

The girl was pale, but she was awake. Her arms, face, and chest were sliced deep. Sticky blood flowed from her wounds, and each second brought her closer to death.

"Please, my daughter fell through the back sliding door," the man cried, pointing to the dying girl with bloody hands.

Jane's memory pulled her back to another time. She knew this girl. She'd seen this girl before. She watched this girl die.

It was a birthday party. Kids, balloons, cake, presents, the whole nine. They were running around the yard playing tag. Running through the house, into the yard, screaming, and having fun. Someone closed the door. It had been freshly cleaned of any fingerprints and grime. She didn't see it. She was too busy watching behind her. She went through it face-first. The glass was so sharp…

Jane fell to her knees in front of the girl, her pants soaking up blood. She began her assessment, looking for the worst cuts of all. They were all bad.

"Please…please don't let me die," the girl moaned from ashy lips. Blood flecked her porcelain skin, which was growing even more pale. The girl cried, silent tears. "It hurts and I'm cold."

Scrambling, Jane looked for something to stem the blood flow. She'd need tourniquets for the arms and heavy towels for the other wounds, at least until an ambulance could get there.

"Hey, get me some towels!" she yelled for the father.

He didn't answer.

Jane looked up, but the man was gone. "Fuck."

She took off her shirt and wrapped it around the worst of the arm wounds. Blood continued pouring out, soaking through the thin material.

"Why can't you save me?" the girl asked, the life fading from her eyes. "Please, I don't want to die."

Jane was crying, squeezing her arm as hard as she could, willing the blood to stop.

"You let me die," the girl said, her voice sounding like she'd eaten a handful of dirt.

Jane was caught off guard. That's not how it happened.

"You couldn't save me. You told me it would be okay, and I fucking died." The girl's eyes were white and she had a smile on her face. "You killed me; now it's your turn."

Jane was frozen. She'd heard of people freezing in stressful situations, but had never felt it herself, until that moment.

The girl reached up and grabbed her by both forearms.

Wincing in pain and shock, Jane looked at the girl's hands and felt herself swoon.

The girl's fingers were gone, replaced with long shards of glass. Each sliver was deep in Jane's flesh. The girl smiled and pulled.

Jane's arms were cut to shreds. For a moment, as she watched the blood flow from open veins, there was no pain. She locked eyes with the girl.

"The dead never die, Detective Wykowski," the girl said. "We never die. We're with you, forever and always." Blood sprayed from her wounds, blasting Jane in the face.

Trying to protect herself from the geyser of gore, Jane put up her bloody arms. Finally, the spray abated, and she looked down at the girl.

She was gone. The only thing that remained was a puddle of coagulating blood and shards of glass.

"No, Myles, no! Breathe, baby, breathe!" A woman shouted from the kitchen.

Jane stood. Her wounds were making her woozy, but she stumbled back into the kitchen anyway. Her arms were like blocks of ice from the blood loss. Her broken fingers were nearly numb, which was the only saving grace of the lacerations.

A boy, no older than four, lay on her kitchen floor. He was wet, only wearing a bathing suit. A woman, his mother, knelt over him, shaking him.

"Breathe, baby!" the manic woman screamed, shaking her unresponsive boy.

Jane's brain felt like it was cramping. A searing pain ripped through her, threatening her thin layer of sanity. This boy…his mother…his cold lips.

She'd only run into the house for a second. Her cell phone was ringing, and she'd left it on the counter. It was only supposed to be a moment and she told Myles to get out of the pool. He was out when she went inside, but her husband had asked her to check something in the basement. Myles was always the impatient boy. She'd forgotten about her son, her only baby. He was on the bottom of the pool when she remembered.

Jane knelt in front of the boy, the mother clutching at her. She was only in her bra since stripping her shirt off to stem the blood flow of the girl in the living room. Modesty was the last thing on her mind.

"Please, Officer, help my boy," the mother shrieked, clawing at Jane.

Jane ignored her, knowing she had a job to do.

Kids, especially drowning victims, have a resilience like no other. Jane began CPR, but as soon as she touched the boy's cool skin, she knew he was gone.

"Did you call 911?" Jane asked, but the mother was gone. She looked around for her, but she wasn't there. Gone like the good dream you were trying so desperately to hold on to. "Fuck," she said, as she continued to press on the boy's chest.

Blood poured from her arm wounds, and she was fading. She was reaching her count of chest compressions and tilted the boy's head back. Her lips pressed against cold ones, as cold as the bottom of a grave. Jane gave a small breath, as not to over-inflate his little lungs. She could taste something, something odd. Bleach.

The boy's eyes sprung open, only inches from hers. They were bone white and had a hint of mischief about them. His little hands, hands that had tried to keep his head above water, clenched the back of her head.

For a fleeting moment, Jane thought back to the scene in the movie *The Sandlot*, where one boy kisses the lifeguard. This was not a movie, and there was no kiss.

The smell of bleach overwhelmed her nostrils, burning them and her eyes.

Myles, his mouth still locked on Jane's, burped once and then vomited right down her throat.

Jane pulled away with everything she had, ripping from the boy's embrace. The bleach burned her throat and she could feel her airway swelling. She scuttled away from him, sliding on the kitchen floor until she hit another cabinet.

Myles stood, his nude chest still and eyes the color of milk. He took a step towards her, a wide smile on his face. His baby teeth were so white.

Her hands pulled at her throat. Blood from her lacerations and broken fingers ran down her chest.

Myles stopped in front of her and squatted down in a very adult way.

"The dead never die, Detective Wykowski." His breath smelled like chemicals. "We never die. We're with you, forever and always."

Jane's world was going black. The last things she saw before the darkness took her were the dead eyes of the little boy.

Mack watched the medical examiners load Jane's body into a body bag. He stared at her pained face as the zipper hissed past her nose.

"How are you doing?" a voice asked from behind Mack.

Mack turned, his eyes red. He sniffled and wiped an errant drop of snot on the back of his hand.

"Hey, LT," Mack said to Lt. Harter. He extended his hand.

Harter took Mack's hand and pulled him in for a brief hug. "We all loved her, Mack," Harter said, releasing his embrace. "But we all know how close the two of you were."

Mack's lower lip trembled. He wanted to speak, but didn't know if he trusted his body. Instead, he nodded and looked away.

Harter watched the medical examiners as they loaded the black body bag with Jane's corpse in it. They set her on a gurney and left the room.

"Suicide, huh?" Harter asked.

Mack looked at him and wiped his eyes. He pinched the bridge of his nose, hoping to relieve some of the tension forming in his brain. "Yeah, looks like it."

Harter looked at the aftermath of the scene.

Shattered glass was strewn about the house, most of it tacky with dried blood. Puddles of crimson soaked into the carpet and stained the linoleum of the kitchen floor.

Harter stared at something else, the bloody glass forgotten—an empty bottle of bleach. "Did she really drink it?" he asked, knowing the answer. "Damn, she could've picked an easier way."

Mack didn't reply. There was no need.

"Hey, guys," one of the other officers called to them.

Mack and Harter both turned, seeing a cop standing on the kitchen threshold. He was young and his skin was pale. Jane's body was the first he'd seen, but it wouldn't be the last.

"Yeah," Harter replied, aggravated by the rookie's interruption.

"I think you should see this." He pointed over his shoulder towards Jane's bedroom.

Mack had no problem leaving the kitchen. In fact, he was ready to leave the scene all together.

He and Harter followed the cop into Jane's bedroom. They froze, looking at the wall.

"The dead never die," Harter said, reading the bloody words written above her bed.

Mack felt like he was going to faint. The writing was hers. The blood ran down the wall in streaks, but he'd know her handwriting anywhere. The darkness was closing in on him, blurring the edges of his vision. The tortured face of his partner flashed before his eyes. The burns on her skin, the broken fingers and the shredded arms. It all hit him like a wave of grief.

No, Jane, they never do. It was his last thought before he hit the ground.

JUST A FRIEND

Kaella Reick was eighteen years old. She was four months into her senior year of high school and had already sucked more dick than she could count. Actually, that's not true. She'd given a lot of blowjobs, but she remembered every dick that had been in her mouth, just not how many times she sucked them.

Right then, a very familiar one was in there.

The Chevy Cobalt was tucked away in a parking lot behind the old bus garage. It was a popular spot for the kids (and sometimes teachers) of Ashmore High School to hang out. Once the new garage was built, the old one became an unused relic. It sat against the Neversink River, which had flooded the building more than once in its forty-five-year existence. Even though it was still usable, the taxpayers were sick of flood damage to vehicles and the building, and a state grant was given for a new one. Everyone was happy, especially horny teenagers looking for a hiding spot after school.

Trevor Felli was thankful for it as he watched the back of Kaella's head work its way up and down in his lap. She was good; no, she was the best. He'd gotten blowjobs from a couple of girls, so he knew bad ones existed. Some girls were terrible at it, thinking it was easy, but not Kaella. She was damn near professional, which was good because he needed to get home soon and couldn't be late.

This wasn't the first time Kaella had blown Trevor. They dated for a few months at the end of their junior year. During that whirlwind of three months, they did every sexual act conceivable, but would fight once the hormones settled. The sex was great, but usually after, they'd fight about something stupid. Then came the party that ended it all.

Kaella knew he was about to blow. She'd been here dozens, if not hundreds, of times with him. Trevor would always start to squirm, as if trying to get away from her mouth; the sensation becoming too much for him. She relaxed, taking the head of his dick to the back of her throat and waited.

"Oh, fuck," he breathed.

A thick spurt of cum shot down her throat, followed by two more in weakening succession. She kept it in her mouth for a second longer; Trevor hated getting cum on his seats. Once he was finished, she licked the last pearly orb from him and smiled. She looked at the clock on the dash as she slid back into the passenger seat. It had only taken her a little over a minute—not bad.

Trevor used a fast-food napkin to wipe her saliva from his balls and threw it in the back seat. He stuffed his still-hard dick back into his pants and zipped them up. "God damn," he said, leaning his head back against the headrest. He had his eyes closed and took a deep, calming breath. "Still the best," he said.

Kaella didn't hear him. She was looking at herself in the visor mirror. Her hair kind of looked cute in the ponytail, but she preferred it down, especially in the winter. She took the elastic band from her hair and put it around her wrist. Her fingers acted as a crude comb, shaking her brown hair out. She could still smell the sweet aroma of her shampoo. Her make-up still looked pretty good, and she didn't look like she had her throat fucked for the last minute. She grabbed her lip gloss from her purse and wet her plump lips. Her lips always swelled just a little after giving a blowjob. She wished they always looked that good.

"So," she said, closing her purse, "what are you doing this weekend?"

Trevor, still riding the high of his orgasm, had his phone in his hands. His fingers flashed and he chuckled. He turned, almost shocked when seeing her. "Huh?" he asked, looking at her side-eyed, and still at his phone.

Kaella turned in her seat. She reached under the radio and turned the heat up. While she was sucking his dick, she was warm, but she was starting to cool down. December in New York could be brutal. "I was just wondering what you were doing this weekend. There's a new slasher movie out and I was thinking about seeing it." She stared at him with her doe eyes.

That would've worked a few minutes before when he was full of jizz, but not then. He clearly didn't give a fuck right then. Trevor's phone went off and he laughed again, fingers flying, then he locked the screen, turning it black.

"Yeah, that sounds cool. I'm not a huge fan of those movies, but I'm sure you'll enjoy it." He tapped the screen of his phone, obviously checking the time. "Laird is having a party Saturday night, so I'm sure I'll end up there. You're more than welcome to come."

Laird Sessions: typical high school asshole. He, like Trevor, was on the Ashmore football team. He wasn't much to look at, unlike Trevor who most girls soaked their panties over, but he thought he was. It didn't hurt he was rich. Well, mommy and daddy were, at least. He always had the best clothes, phones, accessories, and cars. Hell, he drove a nicer car, an M4 BMW, than all of the teachers. He had no qualms about taking advantage of people, especially girls. Kaella had been one of them.

The last time she'd gone to one of his parties, she and Trevor had been dating. Laird's parents were gone, which they often were, and didn't care what he did, social host law be damned. That night, the booze was flowing, and the music was loud. Kaella, like many high school girls, was feeling horny. Trevor's hands were all over her whether they were dancing or just sitting on the couch. She was so wet she was afraid there would be a mark on her jeans.

Trevor whispered in her ear and ran a hand over her crotch, feeling the heat coming off her. He took her hand and led her upstairs. When they opened the door, Laird was there.

Kaella looked at her boyfriend, who was smiling.

"Come on, don't you want to try it?" he asked, his hands under her shirt, unsnapping her bra.

Kaella looked to Laird, who had a maniacal grin on his pimply face and a hand down his pants.

Trevor lifted her shirt over her head and took her bra off. "Atta girl," he said, freeing her perky breasts. He guided her back, her legs hitting the bed.

Reluctantly, she lay down and let Trevor help her out of her pants. Her sex seemed to dry up at the thought of touching Laird, but she could see the excitement on Trevor's face.

"Just a blowjob for him," Trevor said, rolling a condom down his shaft. "That was the deal."

The deal? she thought, like she was a bargaining chip.

Laird pulled his pants down, his uncut dick bobbing as he walked over to her. "Open up," he said, putting his musky crotch in her face.

Trevor entered her as she started sucking Laird's cock.

She kept her eyes closed, willing it to be over.

Laird thrust a few times, causing her to gag, but she kept going. Then, he abruptly pulled out of her mouth. She tried to dodge it, but it happened too fast. He shot a rope of cum on her face and hair.

"What the fuck?" she said, stopping Trevor mid-stroke.

She sat up, wiping the mess from her face. That she didn't care about, it was her hair. It was no treat getting that out, especially at a party. Kids weren't stupid. If she came downstairs with a sticky spot or wet head, they'd know. Her family status already left her on the fringes of popularity, and Trevor was really her only lifeline when it came to popular friends.

"What?" Laird said, smiling as he put his dick away.

"Come on babe, it's no big deal," said Trevor, his dick looking like snakeskin with the condom on.

"Take me home," she said, pushing her boyfriend away. She put her underwear on and got dressed, then stormed out of the room and into the adjoining bathroom, leaving her boyfriend and his erection.

She snapped out of her horrible trip down memory lane. That had been the last time they had sex and broke up the next day. Sure, she'd still blow him from time to time, hoping maybe he'd give the relationship another shot. It wasn't likely. She knew he was toxic, but young love was fickle and hard to deny.

"Oh, okay. Yeah, I'll see," she said, knowing full well she'd never go to that house again.

Trevor looked at her. She still seemed like she wanted to talk, but he really needed to get going.

"Hey, I'm gonna split," he said, checking his phone. "I have to study for the AP Chemistry test on Friday. Actually, you do too."

Kaella rolled her eyes. She was a smart girl, but AP Chemistry was the bane of her existence. If she wanted to get into a decent college, she had to do well on the upcoming test. She knew he was right; she should be studying also, but dreaded it.

"It's only Wednesday. I'll crash study tomorrow," she said. Her mom worked late, so she'd have the place to herself.

Saturday night, her mother's boyfriend, Rick, would be there. Kaella didn't hate him, but he wasn't her father, so he wasn't good enough for her mother. Besides, they fucked like teenagers, especially with a few drinks in them. She would, likely, end up at the basketball game with the rest of the school, and maybe try to tag along with some other girls.

"Yeah, good luck with that," Trevor said. He put his seatbelt on.

Kaella could take the hint. She opened the door and stepped out, putting her coat back on. "See you tomorrow," she said.

Trevor nodded, putting the car in gear.

Kaella shut the door, watching the car drive away. She wrapped herself in her coat, the blustery wind whipping, and started the walk home.

***

Kaella headed towards her locker. She didn't really need anything from it, but she needed to talk to Peter.

All night, she tried studying, but AP Chemistry, especially the upcoming test, had her stumped. Finally, at midnight, she called it quits. Hopefully her brain absorbed enough knowledge to get her through the test. Or, she could go another route, which was her next and final plan.

Peter Mitchel had his head in his locker. He was shuffling through the books he'd need for his next couple of classes. He also grabbed the newest Edward Lee book and stuffed it into his bag, along with a couple of thick textbooks.

"Hey, Pete," Kaella said from the other side of his locker.

He looked around the door. "Oh, hey Kaella," he said, zipping up his bag and shouldering it. "What's up?"

Peter wasn't what many would call a lady's man. He was average height and skinny, but not skinny in the way where muscles showed. No, he was 'skinny fat,' with a little potbelly pressing against his t-shirt, and no muscle tone. He didn't look like he touched a weight in his entire life. Besides that, he wasn't completely unattractive. His shaggy brown hair had a chaotic wave to it, making it nearly stylish. A few years ago, he rid himself of the glasses he'd worn through the earlier grades and gotten contacts. Still, he was lacking in the women department. Over the summer, he'd gotten a dry hand job from Bridgette Kriese, who always smelled like corn chips. She pulled his dick so hard he was sore for a week, his helmet looking like a Christmas light. Still, he'd blown a load, albeit rather painfully. Since then, he'd been back on his perpetual dry spell.

Kaella wasn't the best-looking girl in the school, but she was damn close. Her hair was down again, and she wore a navy-blue turtleneck, which accented her body beautifully. She wasn't the hottest, but the stories about her…prowess… bumped her up a level.

"Have you been studying for the Chem test tomorrow?" she asked, opening her locker as Peter was shutting his.

"Ah, yeah. Of course, I have." He watched her grab a book and shut her locker.

They started walking towards their next class, English Lit, which they had together. A stream of kids flowed through the hallway.

"Right, right." She paused, hoping he'd ask her, but he was focused on not getting shoulder bumped by some asshole jock. "Do you think you could help me out? Maybe give me some pointers?"

Peter looked at her like she had 6 heads. "The test is tomorrow. No amount of tutoring is going to help now."

Kaella grabbed him and pulled him out of the flow of traffic. "Listen," she lowered her voice, getting close to him, "I need to pass this test to make sure I get into college."

Peter began to speak, but she silenced him.

"I know, I know. I waited too late to apply, but I did, didn't I. If I fail Chem, I'm fucked. What can you do to help me?" She gave him her best doe eyes, what she tried with Trevor the day before.

The odd couple garnered a few looks, but Kaella didn't care, and Peter certainly didn't. In fact, being seen intimately close with her could only help him.

Peter's heart was racing; Kaella's breasts were inches away from his chest. He could smell the cheap Chapstick on her lips. For the first time, he realized she had just a slight dusting of freckles on her nose. "Ah, I guess I could try and tutor you a little, but I really don't think that will help."

She licked her lips. Not in an obscene and obvious way, but a subtle, normal flick of the tongue. Moist. Hot. Wet. Her tongue left a slickness of saliva, making her mouth glisten in the cheap overhead lights.

His eyes watched the pinkness flick out like an evil serpent.

"I'll cut to the chase," she said. "If you sit next to me and are a little loose with covering your answers, I'll make it worth your while."

Two things hit Peter's brain at that moment: this girl wanted him to cheat, Peter Mitchel, top of the class. The second was this girl, who was notoriously slutty, was offering something for just a few answers. He needed to play his cards right. He didn't get to the top of the class by being dumb, and knew he was in the driver's seat and needed to act cool.

Canting his head like a dog hearing a whistle, he tried to look shocked, but the grin on his face betrayed him. "You want me to cheat?" he whispered, praying his breath wasn't horrible. "I could lose my scholarship to UB for that." Peter looked around making sure no one, especially a teacher, heard them.

"No, I would be the one cheating. You'd be taking your test as usual. Just make sure your arm isn't in the way."

Peter took a deep breath, as if really perturbed by the whole thing. "Okay, but what's in it for me?"

Yes, Kaella thought. She knew she had him. "Well, what do you want?" she pressed her breasts closer, the padding of her bra touching his chest. She could feel his heart, a bird trapped in his ribs, fluttering. For a second she thought he might pass out.

Just the touch of her bra and thought of her tits made him swell. He hoped to avoid a full-blown erection, because there would be no hiding that. His large brain wasn't his only gift. Peter knew to never make the first offer in a negotiation. Besides, if he was too forward with her, she might bail out. Instead, he shrugged, trying to keep the cool swagger, but the thought of that warm mouth over the head of his cock was almost too much.

Time was ticking until the next class. Kaella had to secure her grade.

"How about I snap you a nude later? No face though," she said.

Peter looked at her, trying to play it off. He'd keep that image in his brain forever, but he knew he could get more. She was desperate. "Kaella, not to be a dick, but this is the age of the internet. If you did send me a real pic, I'm sure it would be great, but I can go online and see whatever I want. Try harder," he checked the time on his smart watch, "and make it quick, class is starting soon."

Fuck, she thought. She, and everyone else, heard about his sandpaper hand job over the summer and figured a tit pic would do it. "Okay, I'll show them to you for real and let you feel them up."

He started walking.

She followed, using her book to press under her breasts, making them stick out.

"That's a good offer, but I don't think it's worth my future. I'm sure they're fantastic though." Peter was getting harder, and he put his left hand in his pants pocket. Using a trick that men for eons had mastered, he flipped his cock into the waistband of his pants so his erection wouldn't be completely noticeable.

She was losing him. They were almost at English class, and it was their last class together.

"Okay," she said, stopping him again, just outside the classroom. She got close, her lips brushing his ear. "I'll suck your dick after school. Is that enough for you to take a risk?"

Peter was full-blown hard and thanked God he was able to get his dick out of the way. He swallowed, his throat clicking, the gentle touch of her lips on his ear leaving him feeling electrified.

She backed away, staring at him. She had him this time.

"Ah, yeah," he stammered, "that sounds much better." He grinned. This would be the longest day in his life.

"One stipulation though," she said.

"Okay." He thought she was going to say something odd, like he had to wear a condom.

"I miss the bus when I... stay late. So, I need a ride home. It's too fucking cold to walk."

"No problem," he said. "I have my grandmother's old LeSabre. I'll take you home."

"Okay, pick me up out front after the last bell." She blew him a subtle kiss and walked into class, Peter on her heels.

The teacher, Mr. Leonard, was talking about Chaucer.

Peter didn't give a fuck about Chaucer, but he did have a plan.

***

For the second day in a row, but with a different guy, Kaella was giving a blowjob behind the bus garage. This one, though, was for the good of her future. When Peter pulled his cock out, she nearly gasped. Who knew the nerdy kid from English and Chemistry was packing a hog? It didn't matter; she worked it like a pro, and within seconds, had a mouthful of warm cum. She opened the passenger side door and spit it out.

Peter was shaking in the driver's seat, his eyes closed.

Kaella looked at his slick penis and wondered how something that big would feel inside her. She began feeling her own heat and moisture between her legs at the thought of sliding down his length.

"Holy shit," he said, breaking her gaze on his member. Peter wrestled his erection back into his jeans, the denim bulging out. "That was awesome," he breathed, finally looking at her.

Kaella was running her hands through her hair. She looked at him and blew a kiss, pursing those plump lips.

Peter grabbed his cell phone from the holder on the dash. He checked it quickly and put it in his pocket, then put the car in reverse and started towards her house.

The first few minutes were silent, and then he spoke. "So, are you going to the basketball game on Saturday?"

She was looking out the window, watching the bleakness of the dawning winter in her town. "Yeah, I'll probably end up there. Not much else to do."

Peter tapped the steering wheel, keeping the rhythm of the song on the radio. "Me too, but I'm not sure how long I'm staying. Bridgette's parents aren't home, so I think we might get some booze and hang out."

The booze might be a few wine coolers or other malt liquor, and their version of hanging out was either video games or a fantasy card game, neither of which he wanted to admit to Kaella.

The steering wheel clicked as he turned onto her road.

Kaella and her mother shared the small house. It wasn't much, and they rented it, but it was enough for them. When Rick, her mother's boyfriend, was over, Kaella wished they had thicker walls, but that was the only downside.

She opened the door. "Thanks for the ride." She slid out of the car, pulling her jacket tight around her. She chewed a piece of gum, the taste of semen long since gone in the minty flavor.

"No problem," he said, looking at the snugness of her jeans. "Thanks for…" *sucking my dick and spitting my cum in the parking lot?* "Ah, just thanks." He looked away from her, feeling his cheeks redden.

She smiled at him. "Let's hope you studied."

Peter smiled back. "Oh, don't you worry. Maybe I'll see you at the game."

"Maybe," she said, closing the door slowly. "Stranger things have happened." She blew him a final kiss and shut the door.

Peter smiled, watching her walk into her house. Greedily, he pulled his cell phone from his pocket and scrolled through. He hoped it worked. He clicked on the video and watched it play, his dick swelling again. Peter knew he was going to have a long night.

***

The basketball game was packed. The gym was sweltering with teenage B.O. and hormones. Everyone in the school was there, even though most of them didn't like the game. It didn't matter; they went to hang out, not to watch.

Kaella was doing just that. She sat talking to a few girlfriends in the bleachers about nothing at all. The final few seconds were dwindling down, and the mass exodus would begin.

Kaella's mother and Rick dropped her off a few hours ago with the promise Shelly, a friend from school, was driving her home. Unfortunately, Shelly wasn't there, but Kaella didn't care, she could find a ride or spring for a cab. As long as her mother didn't find out she lied, she'd be fine.

The buzzer went off, signaling the end of the game. The cacophony of sound was immense. Apparently, their team won, and the crowd began screaming. Kaella joined in to show her undying school spirit.

The teams met at half court and shook hands, then the crowd began to filter out.

"See you Monday," Kaella said to the group of girls she'd been sitting with. They were her first choice of a ride home, but they all squeezed into Rachel's mom's Civic, and there was no way they were fitting her too.

Kaella stood outside of the school, her breath visible in the air. She had the hood of her jacket up to block the wind. A light snow started to fall.

"Hey, what are you doing?" asked a familiar voice.

Trevor stepped into her field of view, his red and black letter jacket making his shoulders look wide.

She closed her phone and put her hand in her pocket. "Ah, nothing. Just waiting for my ride."

Trevor smiled. "I could give you a ride," he said, walking closer to her.

"Yeah," another voice said, "come back to my place. We could all give you a ride." Laird stepped up next to Trevor, along with three more guys from the football team. He held his hands out to them. "We wouldn't mind at all," he said, grabbing his crotch and smirking.

The crowd walking around them watched and laughed.

Someone yelled, "slut," from the anonymous group of kids.

Kaella felt her face grow hot, burning tears threatening to make an appearance.

"Oh hey, there you are," said Peter, walking up next to her. "Are you ready to go?"

The jocks looked at Peter, and back to Kaella, in disbelief.

"Him?" Trevor asked, pointing with his thumb.

"Damn, girl. You will fuck or suck anyone, won't you?" Laird said, getting a high-five from one of the other guys.

Peter blushed. "Our mothers are in the same book club, and Kaella's mom asked me to take her home." He looked away, feigning embarrassment.

Kaella smiled triumphantly. "Yup, I'm ready to go," she said, pushing past Trevor and Laird.

She and Peter walked fast without looking back at the dwindling crowd.

"Here," Peter said, unlocking the passenger side door of the old Buick.

"Thanks," Kaella said, sliding into the cold car, not a moment too soon, as another arctic blast hit the car.

She couldn't help but smile at the small gesture of chivalry. *Maybe I will get to feel that big thing inside me.* She thought about taking Peter's virginity. Hell, she hadn't had sex in a while, just a few blow jobs here and there. Most of the time when she needed satisfaction, she ended up sitting on the shower floor with the detachable shower head between her legs. Those little jets of water could do wonders.

Peter jumped in with an emphasized, "Brrrr," and started the car. He turned the heat on full blast trying to thaw the frosted windshield.

They sat in silence for a second until, finally, Kaella spoke. “Hey, thanks for that,” she said, turning towards him.

Peter was sending a text and then locked his phone. He looked at her; the lights in the parking lot cast shadows on her face. “No problem. Those guys can be assholes and I knew you didn’t want to deal with it.”

His phone went off again. He glanced quickly, smiled, and looked back at her. “Hey, I’m not sure what you have planned for the rest of the night, but me and a couple of people from school are having a little get together at Bridgette’s house.”

Kaella didn’t answer right away. Peter’s circle of friends wasn’t quite her circle, especially Bridgette, who was your typical angry, fat, pretty-girl-hating slob. She more closely resembled a toad than a girl. She was barely 5 feet tall, had a short haircut with the side of her head shaved, a chubby, pimply face, and massive tits that touched her stomach.

The plus of Bridgette was the fact her daddy was a lawyer and had money. Their house wasn’t massive, but they had the newest electronics, streaming services, and usually had booze. The idea of hanging with a few nerds was made a little easier if Kaella could score a drink or two. Besides, she felt obligated since Peter helped her out.

She looked over at him, seeing a growing look of defeat on his face. “Sure,” she said. “I wouldn't mind hanging out for a bit, as long as you can take me home."

Peter perked right up. "Yeah, sure. That won't be a problem." He was giddy, shooting a quick message on his phone. "Okay, let's go."

He put the car in reverse just as a light snow began to fall.

***

Bridgette's house was in a neighborhood like millions of others in America with nice streets, manicured landscaping, and paved driveways. It was a typical, cookie-cutter bi-level.

Peter pulled into the driveway. The snow was falling faster and crunched under his tires.

Kaella noticed only the downstairs of the house had lights on. "I assume they're down there," she said, pointing to silhouettes moving in the lower part of the house. She didn't want to leave the warmth of the car, but once the engine was off, it began cooling fast.

"Yeah," Peter said, meeting her at the front of the car. "Bridgette's parents took her brother to some slasher movie, so they're out for a few hours. She pretty much lives on the bottom floor. It's pretty sweet. She has her own living room, bedroom, and bathroom. The only thing she goes upstairs for is food."

I'm sure that's quite often, thought Kaella, walking toward the back door of the house.

Peter didn't knock, just walked right in. "What's up, bitches?" he said, walking into the living area. He wiped his feet and took his shoes off, putting them in a plastic tray near the door.

"Petey, what's up?" said Josh Celino, who was sitting on an old recliner with a video game controller in his hand. His glasses slid down his nose and with a deft hand, he reached up, pushing them back where they belonged.

Kaella felt out of place, but tried to make the best of it. Her eyes looked around for some kind of alcohol. She went to step in behind Peter.

"Ah, no. Take your shoes off," a shrill voice said from the stairs leading up to the main part of the house.

Bridgette was walking down carrying a bowl of cheese puffs and a 12 pack of beer. She was wearing a skin-tight purple shirt that accentuated every one of her rolls. She had a striking resemblance to Grimace from McDonald's. Her butch haircut was fresh, the sides of her head shaved to the skin, the top long, looking like a duck's ass.

"Oh, sorry," Kaella said, bending over to untie her shoes. She set them in a tray next to Peter's and took her coat off. She looked for Bridgette's guidance on where it went, but the girl was already sitting down to watch the boys play video games.

"Oh, fuck you, you cocksucker," Alan said. He sat on a loveseat, another video game controller in his hand. His fingers blurred over the controller, machine gun bullets flying.

Kaella wasn't a fan of video games, but had to admire the sound quality of the set up. The surround sound made it seem real.

"Here," Peter said, appearing at her shoulder. He handed her a beer and stood at her side watching the video game, which appeared to be ending.

"Thanks," she said, taking the bottle. She looked at him side-eyed. "You didn't drug me, did you?" she asked with a laugh.

Peter smiled and gave her a little laugh, "No, it's all—"

"He wouldn't have to anyway," Bridgette said, her lips and fingers orange from the powdered cheese.

Kaella swallowed her mouthful of beer and looked at the other girl. "Excuse me." It was more of a statement as opposed to a question.

"You heard me," Bridgette said, setting the bowl down and standing up. "I know all about you, little miss slut."

Kaella turned to Peter. "I think you need to take me home now." She set the beer on the nearest end table and started towards her shoes.

"What, you don't think Peter told us about you? How you sucked his cock so you could cheat off his test?" Bridgette laughed, her chins shaking. "Actually, he showed us, not only told us."

Kaella looked back at Peter. "What is she talking about?"

The once-innocent, nerdy kid smirked at her, shrugging his shoulders. His playful, coy grin was vulpine, sly. "Well, I needed a little keepsake from our encounter."

Alan and Josh turned off their game and were watching, smiling.

"Oh, just fucking show her," Alan said. He was the biggest one of the bunch. His mass was well hidden with 3XL shirts, but he was obese.

"Okay," said Peter, taking his cell phone from his pocket.

He touched a few things on the screen, and through the magic of technology, the large TV projected what was on his cell phone.

They all looked at the TV, watching him scroll through his phone.

He opened a video and Kaella instantly felt sick. She watched herself give him a blowjob.

He must've had his phone set up with the screen off, recording the whole time. At one point, he gave the camera a thumbs up and smiled.

She watched herself pause, taking the cumshot into her mouth. She went off-camera, the door opened, and the sound of her spitting his load filled the room.

"Fuck you," she said to him. Her eyes were welled up with tears she, somehow, held back. "I'm out of here," she said, turning towards the door.

Bridgette stood there, her bloated body blocking her escape. "Not yet." Her orange mouth curled in a sneer, crumbs clinging to the wispy hairs on the corner of her lips.

"Yeah, where are you going so fast?" Josh said, rubbing his dick through his pants. "We all just want to have a little fun."

Kaella turned to face him, her back to Bridgette.

"Come on, Kaella, we all heard about your gangbang with the fucking jocks. Why not show us some love?" Peter said, his massive dick bulging in his pants.

Bridgette grabbed her from behind, wrapping her arms around Kaella's, pinning them to her body.

"Let go of me, you fucking cunt!" Kaella thrashed against the soft, hot body of Bridgette.

Peter walked up and punched her in the gut, taking the fight out of her.

Kaella's legs went weak. She felt like puking. Her insides were on fire.

Bridgette lowered her to the ground. "Get her fucking pants off. I want to see this pussy all the boys are talking about."

"You're not the only one," Alan said, a wet spot of pre-cum on his sweatpants.

Kaella began to kick as Peter reached for her pants. "Fuck you!" she thrashed, hoping her foot would find some purchase. "Help, help!"

"Bitch, there's no one here but us," Bridgette said, her cheese-smelling breath in Kaella's face.

"A little help here, guys," Peter said, dodging another kick.

Alan and Josh came over, each grabbing a leg and pinning her down.

Kaella screamed herself raw, tears of fear and disgust running down her face.

"Shhh," Peter said, unbuckling his pants. "Listen, this is going to happen one way or another. Either you let it happen and you walk out uninjured, or you fight and leave fucked up. It's up to you." His dick popped out of his pants.

Kaella once looked at it with heat in her loins, now looked at it in disgust. She did her best to relax, but knew it was going to hurt.

"Atta girl," Peter said, sliding a condom down his cock.

Bridgette looked on. Her lust was growing, hoping she'd get a turn with him next.

Kaella cried as he entered her. What once felt great was a burning fire between her legs.

Peter finished and pulled the condom off, which was full. He upended it on her face. "There, that's for not swallowing the other day," he said.

Drops of cum landed on Kaella as she tried to avoid them.

Alan switched out with Peter. He was much smaller, but it still hurt.

Josh was next. He was done almost as soon as he touched her.

"There," Peter said, throwing Kaella's pants and underwear at her face. "Now you can go." He laughed as Bridgette let her up.

Kaella stumbled, bleeding, into her underwear and pants. "Fuck you all," she cried, fumbling with her zipper. "You'll all be in prison."

Bridgette laughed. "Yeah right, skank. My daddy is a lawyer. Besides, do you think anyone is going to believe you? Especially when the video of you sucking Pete's dick gets out." She laughed. "Just take it for what it is. You're a slut, a plaything. Now, get the fuck out of my house."

Kaella hated them all and their smug faces staring back at her. She knew the girl was right. She could report it, and maybe they'd get in trouble, but the video, and her reputation, didn't help. Besides, they all wore condoms, which would be gone before she left. Hell, they could say she was never there. Peter could tell the police she blew him, and he came on her face, and that was it. She knew her sex was damaged, but without the DNA evidence, nothing would stick.

Kaella stuffed her feet into her shoes without tying them, grabbed her jacket, and stumbled out into the snow.

The snow was falling heavily. Fat flakes fell silently on the already-covered ground. If it wasn't a weekend, the little squall would've surely brought a snow-day.

She was still sweaty from the rape, but the cold air was chilling her fast; faster than she wanted. Soon, she was shivering. Her house wasn't too far away, but in the blistering cold and thick snow, she didn't know if she'd make it. Besides, she was pretty sore and didn't feel like making the long trek home.

She pulled her cell phone from her pocket. She didn't want to call her mother, even though she'd done nothing wrong; victim's guilt was causing doubt. If she saw her mother right then, she'd break down worse than she already was. A tear rolled down her face, birthed not only from the rape, but from the driving cold.

Kaella fished around in her pockets and found a handful of crumpled bills. She desperately needed a ride home, but it couldn't be from someone she knew. She needed to call a cab, get home, shower in scalding hot water, and go to bed. Her icy fingers scrolled through the web browser for a cab number. She called, trying not to shiver.

"Hi, I need a cab from," she looked at the front of the house, "15 Georgian Terrace, to 67 Benson Street."

Kaella sat in silence while the dispatcher on the other line radioed a driver.

"15 minutes?" Kaella asked, echoing what the dispatcher had just told her. "Okay, great. I'll be out front." She ended the call and checked the time.

Desperately, she hugged herself. She fought the urge to look back at the house, but finally gave in.

Warm light radiated from the lower windows. She could only see blurs, but could hear just fine. TV sounds, music, and above all, laughter seeped through the glass. Oh, how she fucking hated them.

Tires crunched on snowy asphalt and Kaella turned, pulled from her reverie. A black car, what some would call a muscle car, sat in the roadway in front of the house. The car was slick like fresh tar. It almost seemed to glow under the streetlights, and the snow slid off it. Even the wheel wells, which were usually a salty, sandy mess, were clear. A black tinted window went down on the passenger side, which was facing Kaella.

She couldn't see the driver, only the glow of a cigarette.

"You need a lift?" the driver asked, turning on the dome light.

An older man sat behind the wheel. He had a blond and white bushy goatee, and wore what Kaella always thought of as an 'Irish' hat, but was obviously bald. His round face and ice blue eyes made him look friendly, but the rasp of his smoker's voice sounded anything but.

Kaella approached the car. She expected it to be loud, figuring it had a big, noisy engine, but she didn't hear a thing.

"Are you the cab?" she asked, looking into the passenger compartment of the car.

It was rich leather all around. An odd, retro looking radio was nestled in the center, the dials glowing red.

"Yeah, sure kid." He puffed on the cigarette, letting the smoke flow from his mouth. It snaked around his nose, kissing his eyes and spreading across the headliner in a hypnotizing pattern.

"Thanks," Kaella said, opening the door. It was the strangest cab she'd ever been in, but it was warm and comfortable. Not to mention, it got her away from that fucking house.

The heat wasn't blasting, but the car was warm. There was nothing blasting from the vents, but it felt like heat came from everywhere. It was an older car, so she didn't think it had heated seats. At that moment, she didn't care, she was just grateful for the warmth.

The driver put the car in gear and pulled away from the house.

Kaella heard the clinking of glass bottles in the back.

"Rough night?" he asked, eyes on the road, cigarette wedged between his fingers.

Kaella picked at her fingers, looking as she peeled a nail off. "Yeah, you could say that." She pocketed the nail, not wanting to toss it on the floor. "Hey, could I bum a smoke off you?"

The driver reached into his shirt pocket (where all old men kept their smokes) and handed them to her.

She looked for a lighter or matches in the pack, but there weren't any.

"Here," he said, pushing a button on the dash. The coiled lighter popped out and he handed her the glowing bullseye.

She had never seen such a thing, and thought it was quite convenient. She touched the tip of her cigarette to the lighter and breathed in. "Thanks," she said, cracking her window.

The bitter cold air consumed the smoke greedily. They rode in silence until he spoke.

"I know what they did to you," he said, eyes on the road. The snow clung to everything, except the car.

Kaella looked at him in shock. "I don't know what you're talking about," she lied, taking a drag. The tip of the cigarette shook.

"Yes, you do," he said, hitting his turn signal. The big car took the turn easily, not even a slip in ever-deepening snow. "I can help you."

Kaella stared at him. His old face, lined with wrinkles, glowed red from the gauges. As if in a trance she said, "Who are you?"

For the first time since driving, he broke his eye contact with the road and looked at her.

"No one important," another puff on a seemingly endless cigarette, "just a friend." He smiled.

She wouldn't quite place his smile as sinister, but it was unsettling, to say the least. She began to weep, rubbing her face with her sleeve.

The smoke was burning her eyes, and she tucked the cigarette through the window. It fell to its death in the snowy road.

"I can help you," he told her, eyes back on the road. He slowed down and pulled over. "We can get them back for what they did to you."

The red light from the radio and gauges seemed to intensify, bathing them in crimson.

Kaella looked through him. They were back in front of Bridgette's house.

"Right now, they're watching the filth of a video, laughing at you, bragging about what they did to you. Do you want to let them get away with that?"

Kaella was still crying, but she wasn't upset, she was scared. "No, I want to hurt them," she moaned. Her voice had an alien sound in her ears.

He nodded. "Good. We can do that." He reached up and turned on the dome light.

The car was lit in bright white, assaulting Kaella's eyes. She squinted as he reached behind the seat.

"Here." He handed her 3 glass bottles filled with gasoline.

She fumbled one, but it was capped. She could only watch, as if in an out-of-body experience.

He took one from her and pulled the cap off. He stuffed the mouth of the bottle with a damp rag stinking of kerosene. He did the same with the others.

Kaella clenched them between her legs as he reached back behind her seat.

Her new friend pulled out an instrument of chaos, oozing death and mayhem—a pump shotgun. The metal was black, and the wood pump and grip were a deep brown.

"Here," he handed her the shotgun.

Kaella took it with revulsion, as if it were a snake. "I don't know how to use this," she said, looking at the gun.

Second-by-second, it became a work of art in her eyes, something nearly sexual in the length of the barrel, the ribbing of the pump-action, and slit on the side. *Sex, sex, and death.*

The old man took a drag of his cigarette. "Don't worry, you will."

"Are there extra bullets?" she asked, caressing the oiled wood and metal. Seconds ago, the thing made her sick, and already, she was asking for more bullets.

"In a shotgun, they're called shells, not bullets, and no, there aren't any extra. Trust me, you'll be fine."

Kaella felt like death on two legs. The Molotov cocktails sitting between her thighs, and the gun in her hands, gave her a God-like euphoria. The pain, shame, and blood-soaked panties were a thing of the past. There was no pain, only fury.

"Oh, here," he pulled a silver Zippo lighter from his pants pocket.

She took it, tempted to try it. She didn't, knowing she didn't have to. It would light on the first strike.

"Are you ready?" he asked.

Kaella nodded slowly, as if in a dream.

The car rolled into the driveway. Snow crunched under the heavy tires as he drove up with the headlights off and came to a stop behind Peter's Buick.

"Good luck, kid," he gave her a little salute as she opened the door.

Kaella had the shotgun in one hand, and a Molotov in the other. The other two incendiaries were in her coat pockets. She walked up to the window and peeked through the sheers. They were all there. She smiled.

The first rag lit. As a guttering flame licked at the soaked cloth, Kaella threw it at the glass with every ounce of strength she possessed. The heavy bottle made short work of the windowpane. It shattered on the ground, bathing the room in liquid fire.

Screams poured from the room as she stalked to the next window on the side of the house.

She set the shotgun down and lit the second one. Just as before, she flung it through a window. It burst into flames, spreading more fire around the room. She peeked through the opening to watch the chaos.

Josh was writhing on the ground, his skinny body consumed by hungry flames. He swatted at his face, each strike pulling scorched flesh from his bones. His hair was gone and scalp a wrinkled, blackened wave of seared meat and bone. The carpet around him was a mat of fire, eating his dying body. Soon, just before his eyes ran watery from his skull, he stopped flailing, waiting to be devoured.

The couch and chair were an inferno. Black smoke started to fill the room and curl out of the windows.

In a moment of brief clarity, Kaella thought the smoke curled like that from her friend's cigarette, only black. Just for good measure, she threw the last one, not bothering to light it.

The fireball ripped through the house. Flames shot from the windows. The vinyl siding began to melt from the heat, curling down the outer walls.

Kaella walked to the back door and waited.

When the door flung open, fat-ass Alan launched forward. His shirt had burned off, leaving a layer of scorched skin. Yellow and black fat peeked from the burns covering his tits. His face was charred, and his left eye was a goopy mess of angry, red flesh.

Bridgette and Peter followed behind him. They were burned, but not nearly as bad as Alan.

Alan rolled in the snow, screaming. His screams were shrill and had an odd note to them thanks to his damaged vocal cords. He thrashed, turning the snow a muddy-red tone. Skin peeled from his body, ripping from the coarseness of the snow and ice. He kept moving, seeking fresh snow, trying to stop the burning, but nothing would give him relief. Well, almost nothing.

Kaella leveled the shotgun, her finger curling around the trigger.

With a hellish bark, it spat buckshot into Alan's gut.

She deftly worked the action, ejecting a spent shell casing. It landed steaming in the snow. She racked the action forward, chambering a fresh shell. Again, she fired, aiming for his face.

In a shower of bone, brain matter, and gore, Alan's head split, deforming his burnt face.

She pumped the gun again.

Peter was on his back in the snow, staring up at her. He tried to slide away; his hands held up in defense.

Kaella aimed the smoking barrel at his crotch and fired.

His groin shredded, blood turning the snow red. Peter screamed, reaching for his ruined genitals, just as the maw of the shotgun was stuck in his face.

Wordlessly, Kaella fired.

Point blank, the buckshot took the top of Peter's head off. The spray fanned out across the reddening snow. Bits of skull, scalp, and brain matter looked like the aftermath of a macabre pinata.

"No, please," Bridgette pleaded. Her legs were a burnt mess. Angry, pus-filled burns covered most of her skin. "It was their idea, honest. They said if I didn't help, they'd do it to me. I swear to God." Snot ran down her face and lips which were still stained orange from the cheese puffs. "Please, please." She stopped, looking at the road. "Mom?" she said as a car approached the house. It was Bridgette's final word.

Kaella put the gun to her neck and fired.

The shot blew a smoking hole in the fat girl's throat. Windpipe, torn arteries, and gristle wept blood down her chest just before she collapsed. Red snow pooled around her cooling corpse.

Kaella racked the shotgun, an empty shell casing landing on Bridgette's body.

Headlights lit up the scene and Kaella turned. She thought it was her friend, but he was nowhere to be seen. Even his tire tracks were gone. The headlights reflected off the fat snowflakes which continued to fall.

A new BMW pulled up behind Peter's Buick and the driver's side door flew open.

"Bridgette!" a man yelled, sliding his way towards the fully engulfed house. His loafers gave him no traction as he fought his way towards the inferno.

"Dad," Kaella yelled from the shadows. She startled herself; she sounded just like the dead girl.

"Oh, my God!" Bridgette's mother yelled as she got out of the car. She didn't fare much better than her husband, slipping and falling on the slick driveway.

Kaella crouched low, hiding in the shadow of a nearby tree. The shotgun felt like an old lover in her hands. She didn't know how many shots were left, but she knew there would be enough.

The father came around the car, seeing the carnage. His mouth hung agape, his brain trying to make sense of the scene in front of him. Finally, all the synapses fired in sync, flooding his damaged mind. "Oh, my fucking God!" he yelled, just as Kaella leveled the muzzle of the gun at his knee.

The blast was so close, the pellets didn't even spread. His knee took the full shot, leaving the bottom of his leg hanging by gristly meat and tendons. Bone even whiter than the snow was visible for just a moment. Then, the blood came.

"Jack!" Bridgette's mother yelled, seeing her husband go down in a heap. She turned and waddled back towards the running car and her son, who was sitting stunned in the back seat.

Kaella fired at the fleeing woman.

A few of the pellets caught flesh, dropping her to the snow.

The overweight woman flailed on the ground, similar to Alan before he died. Hot pellets seared on entry, slowing in layers of fat. She writhed in pain, looking at her horrified son, who still sat motionless in the backseat of the car.

"You created a monster, you pay for the monster's crimes," Kaella said as she shot Jack in the chest, leaving a smoking hole filled with blood.

His heart was demolished, but it still quivered, not knowing it was dead. Blood, already clotting, clung to shattered bone looking like strawberry jam.

Like the predator she'd become, Kaella stalked over to the mother, who was trying to crawl into the car.

One fat hand gripped the handle—her salvation.

Kaella put the gun to the woman's hand and fired.

Fingers and bones flew across the snow-covered driveway in a mist of blood. Bridgette's mother gasped, preparing her body for a feral scream. She didn't get a chance.

With smooth, predatory efficiency, Kaella shot her just under the nose. The buckshot, tight in the plastic wadding, deformed the woman's face, still distorted from the scream that never was. Sirens wailed in the distance, but Kaella barely heard them, just the whimpering from the backseat.

The little boy watched her, her face dotted with bone and blood, as she stalked around the car.

She grinned madly. She was death incarnate.

He was frozen. Warm urine was getting cold in his lap and running down the cracks in the leather seat. His wide eyes looked out the window at the muzzle of the big gun pointed at his head.

Kaella pulled the trigger.

Click.

Flashing lights were approaching. Neighbors were in their windows, some with cell phones in hand.

Kaella racked the gun again, pointing back at the boy. She pulled the trigger.

Click.

The first police car slid onto the street, another right behind it. A spray of snow cascaded over the hood.

She walked past the BMW towards the police car stopped at the end of the driveway. It was obvious the gun didn't want the boy, but she knew it wasn't finished. They were yelling at her, but she didn't care.

Red and white emergency lights lit up the night, reflecting off the still falling snow.

Kaella knelt down, the snow soft and cold underneath her.

The gun wasn't done.

As she opened her mouth, the hot metal of the barrel burned her tongue and tasted oily, almost heavenly.

With just the slightest of pressure, she pulled the trigger.

This time, there was no click.

LOST GIRL FOUND DOG

Becca hated mean people.

The man who put her into the trunk of his car after stuffing a dirty rag in her mouth was mean—worse than mean. The plastic ties he used on her wrists cut the skin and her hands were numb. It was like she had made snowballs with her bare hands and couldn't warm them up.

It was dark in the trunk as it bounced up and down. Her body rattled against the hard surface like they were riding on a trail. Becca liked riding her bike on trails, almost as much as she liked riding the Coasters. That was where she met the man she *thought* was nice.

***

She had woken to a beautiful October day. The leaves were just starting to fall, and it was warm, but chilly in the shade—perfect bike-riding weather. There were a bunch of cool trails behind her house. A long time ago, the town planned to build train tracks, but never finished. They made big hills of dirt, and when the construction was cancelled, the dirt remained, leaving behind a natural half-pipe: the *Coasters* as the kids called it.

Becca got there before anyone else, and was in childhood bliss rocketing up and down the Coasters. Her spokes clicked and clacked as she popped up on the other dirt side, taking a quick spin through a favorite trail of hers, before shooting down the other side. In her mind, she was a pilot fighting aliens.

"Wow, that's pretty cool," a man's voice called out.

Becca slammed her brakes at the top of the hill and looked around. She squinted through the slits of sunlight filtering between the branches and leaves. Her eyes picked him up standing on the other side of the Coasters.

The figure waved and smiled.

Even from far away, Becca liked his smile. It was big, white, and shiny. His blond hair was brushed to one side and looked clean. He had no facial hair, and deep-green eyes that sparkled nicely, just like his smile.

"Are you coming back this way?" he asked. "I want to see it again."

Becca knew she shouldn't; he was a stranger. Though, he looked like a nice stranger, not a mean one. She nodded, her helmet wiggling just a little. She pushed it back into position, gripped her handlebars, and pushed off.

Becca wanted to yell '*wee*!' as she catapulted down the hill, but didn't want him to think she was a baby. Wind rushed by as she defied gravity, going up the other side of the hill. She came to a stop a few feet from him. He was even nicer looking up close.

"Wow, bravo!" He clapped and took a step closer.

Becca smiled at him, pushing back a lock of hair peeking from under her helmet. "Thanks. I've been riding the Coasters for years," she told him.

"Oh jeez, where are my manners?" He stepped closer, almost to the front tire of her bike and held out his hand. "I'm Jasper."

Becca's father taught her to shake hands. He always told her never to shake hands sitting down. She didn't know if a bike counted, but she wanted to be on the safe side. Gently, she laid her bike on the packed earth and reached out to him.

"Becca," she said, taking his sweaty hand.

The change was instant and terrifying. His bright, pretty teeth flashed into a sinister grin. Those green eyes turned putrid and uninviting. Jasper's hand crushed hers in a bone-grinding grip, pulling her into him. He wrapped one arm around her neck and squeezed.

Becca didn't even get to scream as her world went dark.

***

Jasper Jenkins's body shook with anticipation. It had been so long since he had a clean, young girl. He worked on a road crew over the past few years, and been able to satisfy his bloodlust by murdering vagrants and prostitutes. If he had time, and a good spot, torture. It was worth it just to feel their blood and warmth. But he never satiated his greatest desire with them—consuming human flesh.

Sweet little Becca was going to be such a pure treat. *Tender.* His stomach growled with hunger. He had time and a perfect location.

He drove slowly to protect his prize, but there wasn't much he could do to reduce the bumps on the rural roads of Elkpark in upstate New York. He'd searched all along the outskirts of Ashmore, the tiny village nestled between the Neversink and Delaware rivers, searching for a spot. That's where he found the old hunter's cabin.

The car stopped in a cloud of dirt in front of the cabin.

It was ideal for him with only two small rooms and a shallow root cellar with four steps leading down into it. There was no heat, though there was a wood stove, and no electricity or water. It was perfect. Jasper knew having utilities was a luxury, but also produced a bill, which then created a record. That was something he didn't want.

He opened the trunk and looked lovingly at little Becca.

She was sweating and started breathing harder at the sight of him.

Jasper smiled, picking her up like a father about to put her to bed.

She thrashed weakly, but stopped when he pinched her arm. She screamed through the gag.

"Now, that isn't how good girls act," he said, face-to-face with her.

A welt was already rising on her arm.

"If you're a bad girl, I'll hurt you." He smiled. "Understand?"

Becca nodded.

"Good girl," he said, carrying her into the cabin.

The trap door to the cellar stood open and, unceremoniously, he dropped her into the dark hole.

***

Fall in the Northeast is a beautiful time, but it's also deadly. The sun and temperature plummet fast, often catching people unaware. It could be 75 degrees in the sunshine, and within minutes, drop down to 50 or below. Jasper loved it.

He watched twilight descend from the safety of his hideout as a gust of wind whipped against the slats of the cabin. He sat on an old chair, his feet up on a small table. A gas lantern was on the end table next to him, along with a glass of water. An old paperback in hand, he tried to read by lantern light. It wasn't easy, but it was better than nothing.

He closed the book and opened the wood stove, stirring the embers and getting a rise of flame. It wasn't that cold in the cabin, but the fire gave him something else to do besides read and think about Becca. He wanted to start in on her, as he had a new knife, but decided to wait. Jasper didn't mind working in the dark, but seeing their pain and fear was all part of the process, and he didn't think the lantern would give him adequate light for his viewing pleasure. So, he used every ounce of his willpower and waited.

The fire was stoked and raging.

There was a knock at the door.

Eyes snapping and pulse racing, Jasper turned his head. At first, he thought he was hearing things, or maybe the wind had blown something against the cabin.

The knock came again, more forcefully.

Jasper stood, grabbed the fireplace poker, and walked toward the door. His mind was racing on who would be out that time of night, in the middle of nowhere. It couldn't be the police, they wouldn't knock. His door would've been rammed in, and he'd be blinded by flashbangs. Honestly, if they knew what he'd done, what he was, they'd kill him.

"Hello," came a woman's voice. It wavered. "Hello, please let me in." Silence. "I saw you in the chair. Please, I'm hurt and lost."

Jasper relaxed, but not completely.

Fuck, he thought. *If she saw me, then she knows I'm here. If I ignore her, she'll wander away, but if she finds help, they might come back here. If I let her in, people might be looking for her and come here.*

Another idea struck him, one of pure genius.

Or I let her in, kill her and the girl, torch the place, and run away. When someone finds the place, they'll think she was the killer.

It could work.

Jasper flashed a grin and opened the door.

She could have walked right out of his dreams. His eyes took her in from head to toe in an instant, but he savored every detail.

The woman was tall, but not abnormally, about 5'9" if he had to guess. Her dark hair was wet, and wrapped up in a messy bun, accenting her slender, pale neck. She wore a thin button-up, long-sleeved shirt, which was open, revealing a wet, white tank top. Her bra, which was also white, showed through the wet shirt. Her jeans clung to her, also soaking wet.

She shivered in the doorway before walking past Jasper. "Oh, God, thank you," she said, kneeling down in front of the woodstove. She put her hands in front of it, nearly touching the black metal.

Jasper had the poker in his hands as he walked toward her. "Here, let me help you," he said, using the metal hook to open the door of the stove.

A roiling inferno peeked out of the black maw, flames licking at the dying log. He grabbed two fresh ones and slid them in, rekindling the weakening light.

"Oh, that's nice," she said, rubbing herself. "I'm sorry," she stood, facing him. "I'm Talia." She held out her hand.

Jasper took it. He could smell her; a sweetness poured from her like the finest perfume mixed with scents you would find in a candy shop. It was heavenly. He felt himself start to swell. *Maybe I'll rape her corpse after I kill her,* he thought, shaking her powder dry, cool hand.

"Jasper," he said, looking at her wet clothes. "What the hell happened to you?"

Talia laughed and shivered. "Well, I was out for a nice hike with a few friends, but they aren't nearly in as good of shape as I am. So, in my stupidity, I hiked ahead and got myself good and lost. To make matters worse, I fell into the river, destroying my cell phone. It wasn't bad, but then the sun went down." She hugged herself for warmth.

A part of Jasper, an old part, wanted to help her, to give her a blanket or towel…to help her out of her clothes.

She looked into his eyes and smiled. The firelight must've hit just right because, for a second, Jasper thought her eyes turned red.

"Thank God, I found you." She shivered. "I'm sorry to impose, but do you have anything dry I could wear? These wet clothes are killing me."

Jasper was almost in a trance. Her voice was oil on silk, the smoothness caressing his ears. A bead of water ran from her hair, sliding down her neck.

"Ah, yeah," he said.

She followed him into the small bedroom, the only other room in the cabin.

"Here," he said, handing her a t-shirt and sweatpants, hoping they were clean.

"Thank you." She put her hand on his chest.

His heart raced as he stepped out, giving her some privacy. He thought about little Becca in the cellar. He hoped her gag was tight.

***

Becca stopped crying. When the mean man (she wouldn't even *think* his name) threw her in the hole, it hurt. She didn't think anything was broken. That was good; she didn't want a cast for Halloween. It would be too hard to hold her candy.

The hole was small and dark, much darker than the trunk. She could hear the man walking around, but then she heard something else: a knock at the door.

Becca screamed and yelled, but her gag was too tight. It made her choke and cough. Her mouth was so dry, she would've done anything for a drink of water.

The hole smelled like a swamp. It was the same smell as when Becca stepped in black, swamp mud, that rotting stink she hated. After a while, she'd gotten used to it, but then there was a new smell. It smelled like a dog. Not bad like a wet dog, just...dog. She thought she would panic if she were locked away with an animal, especially being tied up and gagged, but she didn't. The smell actually calmed her.

Her mind went back to Halloween and all the candy she was going to get.

***

Talia walked out of the room moments later. Her hair was towel-dried and down, laying damp across her shoulders and upper back.

Jasper could see she had taken her bra off as well. Her stiff nipples poked against the fabric of the t-shirt. Two lovely little tents. He couldn't place her ethnicity, but had a feeling her areolas would be slightly dark. Not brown, but just a deeper shade of pink.

She caught him staring and smiled at him. "I'm just going to set my clothes on the chair to dry." She walked over and grabbed a chair, pulling it toward the woodstove. She draped her clothes over the back of it. Steam rose from them. Her firm ass shook in the sweatpants; she'd taken her underwear off, too.

He felt himself growing hard. He knew he was a good-looking guy, but didn't know if she'd fall for his advances. She also looked like she was in shape and would put up a fight if he tried to rape her. His mind was made up, he'd try to seduce her first. If not, he'd go with plan B.

Talia turned and walked over to Jasper. Her lips seemed fuller, and her eyes darker. "Thank you so much," she breathed, inches away from him. Her breath was sweet, as if she were chewing tea-tree gum. She put a hand on his chest, feeling his racing heart. "I wish there was a way to repay you for your kindness."

Fully erect, Jasper's jeans twisted his hard-on. This was one of the most insane things to ever happen to him, and he'd been a part of some crazy shit. It was like the stories in those seedy porno mags he read as a kid, not real life. A smoking hot woman didn't walk out of the woods, in the middle of nowhere, and fuck. It just didn't happen.

Her hand went to his crotch.

I think it's happening now, he thought.

"Oh, I think *he* knows how I can repay you," she said, rubbing the head of his cock through his pants. She licked his lips, tasting him.

He couldn't take it anymore and kissed her. His ferocity was met by hers, their teeth hitting, but neither caring.

She drove him back, pushing him into the bedroom and onto the bed.

The full moon peeked through the window, a voyeur taking a look. Jasper was thankful for it; he wanted to see this sexual goddess in all her glory.

Talia pulled her shirt over her head, revealing two heavy breasts. They had the perfect amount of natural hang. Her nipples were puckered from the cold and stood straight out, calling to Jasper. She fell to her knees in front of him, her hands rubbing his inner thighs.

"Take these off now," she demanded, stroking his painfully-hard cock.

Jasper's fingers never moved so fast as he undid his jeans and yanked them off. His dick, slick with pre-cum, popped out as he kicked his pants away.

Talia descended on him. She took him in her mouth, taking his length to the back of her throat.

Jasper watched her head bob up and down, her breasts swinging with each movement of it. He ran his fingers through her damp hair, grabbing a handful.

She moaned as he pulled, but didn't break her stride.

Jasper needed to stop her, or he was going to blow his load. He needed her cunt. He didn't know why, but it was almost an animalistic need. There was something about her smell; it was driving him wild.

"Give me that fucking pussy," he said, pulling her hair hard.

Talia looked up at him, her mouth slick with spit and his cock juice. She smiled and stood up.

Jasper removed his shirt, showing off his chiseled muscles.

She looked lovingly at his hard body. "Oh, baby, you have no idea what you're in for." She let the sweatpants drop around her ankles, revealing her sex.

Jasper never thought vaginas to be overly attractive. Many were okay, but it wasn't something he looked at. A lot were razor-burned or too lippy, but not hers. It was the pussy of his dreams. Talia was nearly clean-shaven. No, she had to be waxed. Her lips were bald with not a trace of stubble, only the slightest, most delicate strip of black pubic hair was left.

Stepping forward, her sex opening slightly, a bead of moisture running down the cleft.

Jasper nearly lost his load right there, but held his composure. He lay back, watching her advance, shuddering as she straddled him. Heat came off her vagina as she lowered herself, just touching the sticky tip of his cock.

"You want it?" she asked, staring at him. Her hands reached up and kneaded her breasts.

"You have no fucking idea," he moaned, willing her to descend and take him into her.

Slowly, with expertise, she lowered herself onto him. She shuddered, taking his whole dick to the base.

Jasper let out a sigh. Her tightness was overwhelming. He'd had his share of pussy, but hers felt like nothing he'd ever experienced; it was otherworldly.

Her rhythm was perfect. Sometimes slow, grinding to give her swollen clit some attention, then when her feral lust grew too much, she'd be bouncing, slamming the head of his dick deep inside her.

He was on his back with his eyes closed, willing his orgasm away so he didn't lose it and shoot his wad. Reaching up, his hand touched a soft, yet firm, breast. He teased her nipple, rubbing it between his forefinger and thumb.

"Mmmm," Talia moaned, her hand covering his, rubbing her own breast. She put her free hand on his chest. "Do you like that?"

Jasper could feel his orgasm creeping in. He was almost at the point of no return. A few more thrusts from her sopping wet sex and that would be it. "Fuck yeah," he breathed, opening his eyes to watch. He was buried deep inside her. He could feel her wetness running down his balls and he loved it.

"You've been a bad boy, Jasper Jenkins," she said, staring at him.

"Baby," he said, watching her ride him, "you have no idea." He paused for a second. *How the fuck does she know my last name?*

"You need to be punished." She rode him at a feverish pace, bucking up and down.

That was it. Jasper had reached the point of no return. It was the last, and most painful, orgasm he'd ever have.

Talia's pussy clamped on his cock, holding him in place. She changed in an instant. The fear on Jasper's face was enough for her to cum. Her body quaked as she transformed, waves of pleasure feeding on his horror. Her hand on his chest was no longer thin and delicate, but grotesque and tipped with dagger-like claws. She ripped through muscle and bone, slicing clean through his ribs, but avoided the heart; she wanted him alive just a little longer.

Jasper screamed, blood flowing from his chest. His hand, the one on her breast, grasped coarse, black fur. He tried to pull it away, but it was caught in her vise-like grip.

She broke his wrist backward. Tendons and shattered bone poked from his skin.

He wailed just as his orgasm reached its crescendo. He couldn't help it, his body just reacted. The pleasure and immense pain were hot and cold, sweet, yet bitter. A fierce blast of cum pumped into the beast on top of him.

Talia's face morphed, too. Her smooth skin was ridged, new bones growing underneath the old. Her mouth elongated until it was impossibly wide. She took his broken arm and bit down, severing it above the elbow. A gout of hot blood shot onto the wall, the brachial artery ripped to shreds. Her mouth slick with gore, Talia smiled.

With both hands and her mouth free, she attacked in earnest. Razor sharp claws ripped the rest of his chest open. She spread his ribs, exposing the still-beating heart. The organ fluttered; it was in panic mode as it tried to pump blood to the dying body. Its efforts were in vain.

Ripping it free, she devoured it in one bloody bite.

Finally, the light went out of Jasper's eyes, but Talia was far from done. She opened his gut. The stench of stomach matter and shit filled the air. To her, it was like perfume.

Talia fed ravenously.

Becca woke up. She didn't mean to fall asleep, but she was so tired.

In the moments before she was fully awake, she thought her room smelled funny. Her eyes fluttered open, and she panicked. She wasn't in her room at all. *The hole*. She was in a dirt hole because some meanie weenie threw her in there. She put her hands to her mouth to stifle a cry.

My hands, she thought, *they're free.* She looked at her wrists, which were cut from the plastic ties, but unscathed. Her feet were also free, and she was ungagged.

A bar of morning light shone through the trap door where the man had thrown her. The door was open, revealing a steep ladder. Something walked into the light, and Becca shrieked. She caught herself, not wanting to let the man know she was awake.

It was a dog. The dog sat in the light, its tail wagging. Her black fur looked like oil in the light.

Becca put a hand toward the dog, hoping she wouldn't bite.

The dog let out a happy yip and walked over to sniff her hand. The cold nose felt nice. Then she licked her fingers, tail wagging the whole time.

"Shhh," Becca told the dog. "There's a mean man upstairs." For some reason, she didn't think that was true any longer though. Something felt different.

Walking away, the dog mounted the ladder. With a step and a hop, the dog went up, looking down at Becca.

Becca stood on wobbly legs and climbed out. The only other door in the cabin was shut, and this made her happy. A very bad smell was coming out of there.

She petted the dog, who looked up at her. "Come on, let's get the hell out of here," Becca said. She thought her mommy and daddy would forgive the bad word.

Becca never had a pet before. Daddy was allergic to cats and mommy hated dogs. She thought her mommy might make an exception for this one.

The pair walked away from the cabin, a girl and her dog, toward the sounds of traffic.

ABOUT THE AUTHOR

Daniel J. Volpe is the splatterpunk award-winning author of PLASTIC MONSTERS. His love for horror started at a young age when his grandfather unwittingly rented him "A Nightmare on Elm Street." Daniel has published with D&T Publishing, Potter's Grove, The Evil Cookie Publishing, and self published. He can be found on Facebook @ Daniel Volpe, Instagram @ dj_volpe_horror and Twitter @DJVolpeHorror Signed books can be found at djvhorror.com

Made in the USA
Middletown, DE
25 January 2025